The Atlantis Stone

by

Alex Lukeman

The Project Series:

White Jade
The Lance
The Seventh Pillar
Black Harvest
The Tesla Secret
The Nostradamus File
The Ajax Protocol
The Eye of Shiva
Black Rose
The Solomon Scroll
The Russian Deception
The Atlantis Stone

The PROJECT is a covert counter terrorism and intelligence unit answering only to the President of the United States.

The Team

Elizabeth Harker: Director of the Project. Formerly part of the task force investigating 9/11 until sidelined for challenging the findings. Picked by the president to head up the Project because of her independent thinking and sharp intelligence.

Nick Carter: Former major, USMC. The team leader in the field, with years of combat experience. Suffers from PTSD and nightmares. He's got it more or less under control.

Selena Connor: A renowned expert in ancient languages. Accomplished martial artist. Independently wealthy, the result of an inheritance.

Lamont Cameron: Former Navy SEAL. Expert in all things water related. His irreverent attitude sometimes drives Elizabeth Harker to distraction. A tough cookie.

Ronnie Peete: Nick's oldest friend and a fellow RECON Marine. Expert with explosives, weapons and all things mechanical. A full blooded Navajo, Ronnie brings a solid approach and the wisdom of his culture to the team.

Stephanie Willits: Elizabeth Harker's deputy. A world class hacker, Stephanie maintains the Project's Cray computers. She is responsible for the satellite communication network that keeps Harker up to speed during missions and the team connected to home base when they are in the field.

Prologue: Alexandria, Egypt
1801 C.E.

Besieged and surrounded, there was nothing left to do but surrender.

Two men sat on the veranda of the villa Napoleon's commander in Egypt had commandeered for French Army headquarters. General Abdullah Jacques-François Menou poured two glasses of cognac and handed one to the balding, round faced scholar sitting across from him.

Geoffroy Saint-Hilaire had been part of the campaign from the start. He'd collected a large selection of fossils, artifacts and native plants for shipment back to France. But now the British were demanding that everything be turned over to them before they would lift the siege. They wanted the stone found at Rosetta.

The stone was part of a granite stele erected by King Ptolemy V with a proclamation inscribed upon it in three different scripts; hieroglyphics, demotic and ancient Greek. It meant Egyptian hieroglyphics could now be translated, using Greek as the key. It was a major archaeological find and the British were determined to have it.

What the British didn't know was that there was another discovery, a tablet inscribed with an unknown language. It had been found hundreds of kilometers west of Cairo. Strangely light in weight for its size, two men could lift and carry it. Saint-Hillaire intended to study the Rosetta stone until he understood the hieroglyphics, then turn his attention to the second.

"I won't give them what they want," Saint-Hillaire said. "I will destroy everything before I'll let them have it."

"The stones are just stones, Geoffroy."

Saint-Hilaire looked at his friend as if he'd just spit in the baptismal font at Notre Dame Cathedral.

"The British will have their way," Menou said. "They don't know about the tablet. We can't make sense of it anyway. It's worthless."

"Just because we don't understand it doesn't make it worthless. It's at least as old as the stone we found at Rosetta, perhaps older. I will not give it up, not to those bastards."

Menou lifted his glass and drained it. "Geoffroy. My men are dying. We are without rations. The Arabs sneak through the streets at night cutting throats. I must surrender. There is no choice."

Saint-Hilaire was becoming angry.

"Yes, but you can negotiate. Give them the stone from Rosetta if you must, to satisfy their greed. I've made impressions of everything on it. But I will keep the other. I demand that I keep my natural history specimens. If they refuse, I will destroy them all."

"Calm yourself, *mon ami*. I will do what I can. The British want to get this over with as much as we do. Go ahead and hide your tablet."

The scholar took a deep breath, mollified. "We must preserve as much as we can. God knows, we have nothing else to show for Napoleon's ambition."

"Bonaparte is a great general. His tactics and formations have changed the face of modern warfare."

"He is a great general who led our Army to destruction and ran for home when things became difficult. Now that he is First Consul, I fear for our Republic."

General Menou poured another glass of cognac. "Bonaparte is a patriot who will guide France to greatness. It would be best if you kept your opinion to yourself."

"Perhaps." Saint-Hilaire rose. "Now you must excuse me, Baron. There is much to do before the British enter the city."

Menou stood. "Move quickly. General Hutchinson grows impatient. If he finds the tablet I will not be able to keep him from seizing it."

"He will not find it. I can assure you of that."

Once outside Menou's headquarters, Sainte-Hillaire hurried toward the sheds where his beloved specimens were stored. The August sun burned down from a relentless sky filled with fire. His white linen shirt was damp with sweat by the time he got to his destination.

The wooden shed was over a hundred feet long, open on the ends. Even under the shade of the peaked roof, Saint-Hilaire felt like he was standing in an oven.

I'll be glad to see the last of this miserable heat, he thought.

Narrow aisles snaked between wooden crates stacked along the length of the shed. They held everything gathered during the years of conquest and retreat. Two of Saint-Hilaire's assistants stood watching over workers sorting out the cases of specimens. He called out to them.

"François, André, come with me."

The two men followed him to the far corner of the shed, where the Rosetta find stood upright on the dirt floor. Next to it was a long crate.

Saint-Hillaire motioned at the crate. "Open it."

François pried the lid off the crate. The tablet lay inside, under a layer of packing straw.

"Take out the straw and fill the crate with dirt. Plant native flora in the earth. Once you've done that, put the crate with the live specimens we're sending back. Leave it open so the British can see it's only plants."

"But the tablet will get dirty," André said.

"You are an idiot. Of course it will get dirty. We'll clean it off when we get home."

François snickered.

Sainte-Hilaire was allowed to keep most of his specimens but it wasn't until January that the crate with the tablet was loaded on a ship bound for France. Once he arrived in Paris, the historian had all of the crates taken to the Natural History Museum on the left bank of the Seine.

The next night he ordered the tablet uncovered and moved to the basement, away from the rest of the Egyptian specimens. He intended to have it taken to his château for personal study.

Time and events intervened. The tablet remained where it was. The room became a storeroom for the museum's disused things. No one paid any attention to the odd stone tablet leaning against the back wall.

That was because they couldn't read what was on it.

CHAPTER 1

Time was running out for Yuri Sokolov.

Sokolov sat in a shabby room in a third rate hotel in Amsterdam, writing a letter. He scrawled his signature at the bottom of the page and placed the letter in an envelope, along with an old map and a faded photograph. He sealed the envelope and wrote the address. He added a stamp.

Bracing himself against the battered wooden end table he'd been using for a desk, Sokolov rose, wincing at a pain in his hip. He turned off the light and moved to the window. Careful to stay to the side, he pulled back a flimsy curtain and looked out onto the street and canal three stories below.

It was past midnight. On the other side of town, in the red light district, there were crowds and police everywhere. In this part of the city the streets were deserted. All the good citizens were in their beds.

Yuri wasn't looking for good citizens.

He couldn't see anyone watching. A flicker of hope fluttered in his chest. It was possible they didn't know where he'd gone when he left Moscow.

The postbox was two blocks away, next to a newsstand on the other side of the canal. He shrugged on his long overcoat, thankful for the warmth of the fine wool fabric. He stepped into the hall and closed the door to his room behind him. The elevator was broken, forcing him to take the stairs. They were narrow and poorly lit. His heart pounded against his ribs as he thought about who might be waiting for him on the next landing. On the ground floor, the concierge slept in his metal cage. Yuri slipped out the entrance into the raw night. A thin mist shrouded the city.

He glanced to the right and left. *Still no one.* Wisps of fog rose from the black waters of the canal. He hurried to the footbridge spanning the canal and crossed to the other side, his footsteps sending muffled echoes from the sleeping buildings lining the canal.

Sokolov's destination appeared in the mist. The stand was closed at night but the bright orange TNT box was on the outside, where he could get rid of his burden. With a gasp of relief he reached the box and thrust the envelope into the left-hand slot, reserved for mail leaving the country.

Now he would go back to his room, gather his few things together, and head for the train station. By tomorrow he would be in Paris.

The concierge was nowhere to be seen when Yuri entered the hotel. The lift was still broken. He began the climb back to the third floor.

Later, when the police questioned the other guests of the hotel about events that night, no one had anything useful to say about the man in room 314. No identification had been found on the body. No one had heard cries coming from the room, though the victim had been brutally tortured before he died. The only other occupant of the third floor was an elderly lady who kept asking investigators to repeat what they'd said.

A tenant on the second floor reported loud music playing for a while but had heard nothing else. Nobody knew anything, which was often the case in hotels where the residents wanted to avoid the police at any cost. The arrests of a minor drug dealer and a petty thief were small compensation for the failure to identify either the murder victim or his assailants.

The morning after the murder, the postal box was emptied. The envelope was sent on its way to America.

CHAPTER 2

"Ouch."

Nick Carter set his razor down on the edge of the sink and dabbed at the cut with a shred of toilet paper. He gave himself a once over in the mirror. The nightmares had started again. He wasn't sleeping well. Dark shadows under his eyes brought out their gray color and the flecks of gold hidden in them.

A fresh shave, and he could already see the next beard ready to spring out. Sometimes he wondered why he bothered. His face was still pretty much the way it had been yesterday, barring the cut making a red spot in the bit of white paper he'd laid on it. It was a strong face, not particularly handsome, but not ugly either. He thought he could see some new signs of aging. Or was he imagining it?

He needed a good workout in the Project gym, something to relieve the tension he'd been feeling for the last few weeks. He wasn't sure where it was coming from.

It was early morning on what promised to be a beautiful spring day in Washington. Nick dressed in comfortable slacks and a light gray cotton shirt. He walked into the kitchen, took a cup from the cabinet and filled it with black coffee from a pot brewing on the counter. He took the cup over to a table littered with mail delivered the day before, sat down and started sorting through it.

Selena came into the kitchen. She poured a cup and joined him.

Selena was a woman people noticed. She had intense eyes that changed color from violet to deep blue and back again, depending on the light. Either way, they were a perfect match for her red-blond hair. Two inches shorter than Nick's six feet, she was sixty pounds light of his two hundred. The amount of body fat on her didn't amount to much but it was there in the places where it mattered.

"You have a letter from Amsterdam." Nick passed it over. "Your agent sent it over. It's addressed to Selena Connor."

There was nothing unusual about getting letters using her maiden name. Selena still corresponded with some of her former academic acquaintances. Sometimes she got invitations for appearances and guest lectures, though there were fewer of those these days. She usually had to turn them down. It had been some time since she'd last given a formal lecture, but her international reputation as an expert in ancient languages still brought requests. They came by way of an agent who handled professional correspondence for her.

"Amsterdam? I don't think I know anyone there. It's probably someone who wants me to give a talk."

"There's no return address."

"That's unusual. Let me see it."

The only writing on the envelope was a spidery scrawl with her name and the address of her agent. She used a table knife to slit open the envelope.

"It's an old photograph and a map. And a letter."

"A map of where?"

She unfolded the map. It was creased and worn, as if it had been carried in someone's pocket for many years.

"Egypt, when it was still a British protectorate. That would be the first part of the last century."

She set the map aside and picked up the photograph. It was yellowed and torn on one corner.

"What does the letter say?"

"I'll read it out loud."

Dear Dr. Connor,

My name is Yuri Sokolov. I am a senior researcher at the Russian Academy of Sciences in Moscow. My field is Middle Eastern archaeology. I am writing to you because of your unique reputation as an expert in Linear A.

"A Russian?" Nick said.
"You're interrupting."
"Sorry."
Selena continued reading.

The photograph was taken sometime in 1912 by Mikhail Popov, an archaeologist friend of Czar Nicholas III. I found it in a file of Popov's correspondence, along with the map of Egypt. There's a mark on the map near the coastal city of Marsá Matruh. I suspect that is where the picture was taken.

Selena picked up a magnifying glass and studied the picture.
"Interesting," she said.
"What's interesting?"
"It's a picture of a stone pillar, lying in sand, inscribed with hieroglyphics and what looks like Linear A. I've never seen those two languages combined before. It has to be very old."
She turned back to the letter.

You can see two kinds of writing on the pillar in the photograph. The hieroglyphics are a very early style. The other is a variant of Linear A.

I was able to translate only part of the inscription but was greatly surprised by what I discovered. I gave a copy of the picture to a colleague, seeking a second opinion. That was a mistake. There have been rumors my colleague is an informant for the security services. The same evening a friend called to tell me the FSB were on their way to my apartment.

What is inscribed on the pillar has possible military implications, enough to explain FSB interest. My government cannot be trusted to make this information public. When you translate it you will understand my concerns.

I am going on to Paris tomorrow and from there to America. I would like to meet with you and discuss this with you in person.

Cordially, Yuri Sokolov

"He sounds like an idealist," Selena said.

"That's it?" Nick asked.

"That's all there is."

"What kind of military implications?"

"He doesn't say."

"Can you read the script in the photograph?"

"Let me take a look."

Selena got a pen and paper and began studying the picture through her magnifying glass. Nick watched her making notes. Her expression was intense, focused.

She said, "If this says what I think it does, you're not going to believe me"

"Try me."

"I think the inscription is about Atlantis."

"You have got to be kidding."

"See? I told you that you wouldn't believe me."

"Atlantis is a legend."

"If it turns out that it isn't, a lot of people are going to get upset. Egyptologists, for example."

"Are you sure it's about Atlantis?"

"I'm not certain, but it's a good bet." She pointed at the photograph with her pencil. "These characters form a phrase that means homeland. It's described as a plain and mountain surrounded by water."

"That could be about Crete. The Minoans used Linear A and Crete isn't that far from Egypt. What else does it say?"

"It's an account boasting about the power of the homeland. It says the priests lifted heavy blocks of stone into the air using an object given to them by the gods, an artifact of some kind. "

"A force that could lift heavy stones? Thousands of years ago?"

"That's what it says."

"That must be what Sokolov meant about military implications. If the Russians think there's anything to this, they wouldn't want him telling anyone about it."

"I wonder if he's in Paris?"

"I doubt it. It must've taken days for that letter to get here. Then it had to go through your agent to you. If he'd followed through on his plan he'd be here by now. He would have contacted you."

"You think they caught up with him?" Selena asked.

"If they did, it wouldn't be good news for him."

"If he's a senior researcher with a prestigious Russian Institute, he'll be in the database. Steph can look him up."

Stephanie Willits was Director Elizabeth Harker's deputy, in charge of the Project computers. If what you wanted was in a database somewhere, Stephanie could find it.

"We'll ask her when we go in."

Selena's voice was enthusiastic. "We should look for that pillar. There's more written on the back where I can't see it. It might tell us more."

"Does the map show where it was photographed?"

"Not exactly. Marsá Matruh is on the Mediterranean coast west of Cairo. The spot on the map is farther on, toward Libya. "

"I don't think foreigners are popular in that part of the world right now. It won't be easy to get to it."

"If it led to discovering the force mentioned in that inscription, any effort would be worth it."

Nick reached up to scratch his ear but thought better of it.

"I suppose so," he said.

CHAPTER 3

Elizabeth Harker opened the French doors onto the patio outside her office and contemplated the day ahead. Security be damned, it was too nice a day to leave the doors closed against the spring air. Later it would be humid and hot. This early in the morning, the breeze was cool and fresh. The scent of flowers and new grass drifted into the room.

Birds sang and chirped outside. She hoped the cat didn't catch one and bring it to her as a gift.

Usually she dressed in a black pantsuit and white blouse. Today she'd reversed the pattern. The suit was white, the blouse black. A gold and emerald pin in the shape of a Celtic knot graced her left breast. The emeralds picked up the vibrant green of her eyes.

Elizabeth liked to dress in black and white. It kept things simple. Her life was complicated enough without worrying about what she was going to wear. The habit had started when she was in law school and carried over when she went to work for the Justice Department.

She'd been part of the 9/11 task force but as the investigation progressed, she'd become uneasy and then concerned. She'd argued with the conclusions being fed to the media and the public about what had happened. Elizabeth was branded as someone who wasn't a team player and transferred to a dead-end job on an endless RICO investigation. She'd been about to resign when President Rice tapped her to head up the Project.

Rice had a problem with the intelligence agencies. Sometimes they thought they knew better than the White House what needed to be done. Critical information was withheld because someone decided Rice had no need to know. How the hell was he supposed to make good decisions when he didn't have all the facts he needed? He'd wanted a new agency that answered only to him. He'd wanted it small and out of the public eye, with someone to run it who would tell him the truth. It was Harker's maverick refusal to go along with the official story about 9/11 that had caught his eye

Elizabeth had built a team she was proud of, led by Nick. He was the first person she'd recruited, right out of a hospital bed in Bethesda. Sometimes he'd been difficult to handle but she'd never regretted the decision.

Selena entered the picture when her wealthy uncle was found tortured and murdered. A personal friend of the president, Rice asked Elizabeth to look into it as a favor. Events piled on one another and now Selena was part of the team. She'd earned it, the hard way. She had the bullet wounds and scars to prove it.

The other two members of the field team were Ronnie Peete and Lamont Cameron. Both had been badly wounded in Germany during the last mission. Ronnie had been a Gunnery Sergeant in the Marines. Lamont had been a Navy SEAL before coming to the Project.

Elizabeth worried about them. Years of wounds and surgeries were beginning to take a toll on their bodies. It was true for Nick as well. Selena had never been in the military but after few years in the Project she was catching up to the others.

The team always seemed to find the sharp end of the sword. Elizabeth prayed they would all continue for a while longer. She couldn't imagine replacing any of them.

The last piece of her team was Stephanie Willits. Steph was as good with the computer as the others were with their weapons. With Steph at the keyboard, the Crays downstairs were a powerful resource at Elizabeth's command. If there was anything Stephanie couldn't do with a computer, Elizabeth didn't know what it was. She was essential to the success of the Project.

Stephanie walked into the room.

Elizabeth said, "I was just thinking about you."

"Nothing bad, I hope."

"Not at all. I was thinking how grateful I am that we work together."

Steph smiled at her. "It's mutual."

"You look chipper today," Elizabeth said.

"I think Lucas and I have finally gotten past what happened."

What had happened was a highway ambush by assassins trying to take out the team. Three months pregnant, Stephanie had lost the baby. Lucas Monroe was the Director of Clandestine Services at Langley and her lover. He'd been driving the car and seriously wounded at the same time. The aftermath had been days of dark depression and grief.

"We're going to try again," Stephanie said. "The doctor said there's no reason we couldn't have another child. We weren't ready before now." She paused. "I wasn't ready."

"Steph, that's wonderful. I'm so happy for you. I think it's the right thing for both of you."

"What's on the agenda this morning?"

"Nick and Selena will be here any moment. Ronnie and Lamont are over at Walter Reed for checkups. For once there doesn't seem to be a fire we have to put out."

"That won't last long," Stephanie said. "We'd better enjoy it while we can."

"We haven't done anything together for fun in quite a while. I thought we could all have lunch at that new restaurant in Georgetown. If we go early enough, we'll get a good table."

"That's a great idea," Nick said through the open door.

He came into the room with Selena. They took seats on a long leather couch facing Elizabeth's desk.

"Where are Ronnie and Lamont?" Selena asked.

"Getting checked out at Walter Reed."

"What are we looking at this morning?" Nick asked.

"I was just telling Steph things are quiet."

Selena said, "This may change that."

She handed Sokolov's letter with the map and photograph to Elizabeth.

Stephanie said, "I told you it wouldn't last long."

Elizabeth examined the photograph.

"A stone pillar? What's that on it?"

"Two kinds of writing. An early version of hieroglyphics and a variation of Linear A. That picture was taken in Egypt. I've only made a partial translation but I think we have to follow up on it."

"What does it say?" Steph asked.

Selena told them what she had gotten so far.

Elizabeth looked at her as if she'd been smoking something.

"That is the most bizarre thing I have ever heard you say. This inscription is about Atlantis?"

"It's possible."

"Why do you think that? It could be about the Minoans. They were surrounded by water."

"That's what Nick said. That would make sense except for the part about moving heavy stones using an unknown force. Judging from the letter, the Russians are taking it seriously. That's why we have to pay attention. We need to look for that pillar."

Stephanie said, "What if this Yuri Sokolov isn't who he claims to be? The letter could be misdirection on the part of the Russians."

"Why send it to Selena?" Nick asked.

"It could be a trick to draw the team out."

"And I thought I was paranoid."

Steph played with gold bracelets on her left wrist. "You know they'd love to create trouble for us."

"Sure, but there are easier ways to do it."

Elizabeth said, "Steph, see what you can find out about Sokolov. Also the friend of the Czar mentioned in the letter. There might be a record of him."

"I'll get right on it."

"Selena, how long will it take you to translate the rest of that inscription in the photograph?"

"I don't know. I'll start working on it right away."

There goes lunch, Elizabeth thought.

"I guess I'll have to settle for that."

CHAPTER 4

General Alexsandr Volkov looked down from the window of his office on the top floor of FSB Headquarters in the old Lubyanka prison, contemplating the statue of Felix Dzerzhinsky dominating Lubyanka Square. Volkov's hands were clasped behind his back. His fingers moved with restless energy. The Director of the FSB was a broad block of a man, with hairy arms and the build of a wrestler. Behind his back he was called The Gorilla. No one ever called him that when he was within earshot.

Volkov's job as head of the *Federal'naya sluzhba bezopasnosti Rossiyskoy Federatsii* made him a powerful man in Russia. The old Committee of State Security, the KGB, had been broken up into separate organizations after the fall of the Soviet Union. FSB was in charge of internal state security and intelligence gathering. External security and foreign intelligence was the responsibility of the *Sluzhba vneshney razvedki*, SVR.

Volkov's world would have been perfect if foreign intelligence was under his control. Since it wasn't, he settled for doing everything he could to undermine SVR and its new director, Alexei Vysotsky. His ambition was to resurrect the KGB as it once was, with himself in command. The name would be different, of course. Whatever the name, the function would be the same. But it would require the blessing of the Federation president, Vladimir Orlov.

Orlov meant *eagle* in Russian; Volkov meant *wolf*. There was no doubt in Volkov's mind that one day the wolf would pull the eagle from the sky. In the meantime, he had to play the role of loyal officer and servant of the state.

A report lay on his desk about the interrogation of Yuri Sokolov. His agents had been thorough, if too enthusiastic. Better if the traitor had been brought back to Moscow for more extensive questioning, but the questioning had been too much for the old man. Even so, enough had been learned to justify further action.

Sokolov had talked about the pillar in the photograph he'd given to Volkov's informant. He'd babbled about the writing on it. He'd talked about Atlantis and a power that could lift stones in the air. Volkov didn't give a shit about Atlantis. All he wanted was more information about the artifact that controlled that mysterious power.

Sokolov had told Volkov's interrogators there was a map showing where the pillar had been photographed. He'd sent it with the picture to America.

The FSB was not supposed to intervene on foreign soil. That was the job of SVR. But like the American FBI, the FSB could legally make an exception when a Russian citizen was involved. Sokolov had been a Russian citizen. As he saw it, Volkov was within his mandate to pursue the issue, wherever it took him.

He turned away from the window, sat down at his desk and opened the folder with the report. Sokolov had revealed where he'd sent the picture.

It complicated things.

Selena Connor was part of the Project, red-flagged in the database of every Russian intelligence agency. That was where it got complicated. She wouldn't be easily intimidated into handing over the map and picture. He needed that map.

It might be possible to steal them without confronting her, Volkov thought. *If not, I'll have to take extreme measures.*

As long as the FSB didn't bring down the wrath of the Americans on the Kremlin, no one in Moscow would mourn the death of an American spy.

Volkov didn't know if the force described on the pillar existed, but if there was any chance it was real he had find it before the Americans did. With the map, he could find the pillar and that might tell him more. If he could discover the secret of the force and how it was controlled, he'd gain allies in the military and among the oligarchs. He'd gain favor with Orlov. It would put him in a better position to make his move against SVR and Vysotsky.

He pressed a button on his intercom.

"Get Major Yeltsin in here."

"Sir."

Five minutes later there was a knock on his door.

"Enter."

Major Borya Yeltsin wore a reasonably good dark suit, white shirt and black tie. Unlike SVR, officers in the FSB wore civilian dress rather than army uniform. Yeltsin was dressed in civilian clothes, but no one would mistake him for a civilian.

His hair was cropped close to his head and high on the sides. He had the kind of unsmiling eyes found in soldiers who have seen the red edge of war. Broad shoulders and chest showed that he worked out on a regular basis. Yeltsin stopped in front of Volkov's desk and snapped to attention.

"You sent for me, sir?"

"I have a mission for you. I want you to take a team to America and retrieve something for me."

"What is it you wish me to obtain?"

"A picture and a map. They were sent to a woman who lives in Washington. She is a member of one of their covert intelligence units. Try to recover the items without involving her in a direct way. If that is not possible, you are to take any action necessary to ensure the success of your mission."

Volkov handed a folder to Yeltsin, along with a copy of the photograph.

"I want you to bring back the original of this photograph and a map that accompanies it. The map will date to the late nineteenth or early twentieth century. It should be easy to identify. The address where everything was sent is in the folder, along with a picture of the woman and a summary of who she is. Do not underestimate her. She is part of a direct action team, highly trained."

"She's a woman. I can handle it."

"Don't let your balls get in the way, Major."

Yeltsin stiffened at the rebuke. "Sir."

"This mission requires discretion. It would be much better if you avoid any wet stuff but if it comes to that, make sure you are not apprehended. There must be no trace of our involvement. Understood?"

"Yes, sir."

"Pick your team and let me know when you are ready to leave. Make it soon."

"I can leave later today."

"Excellent. Dismissed."

Yeltsin snapped his heels together and left the room.

As he walked down the hall he looked at the picture of Selena.

An attractive woman, he thought. *It would be interesting to interrogate her.*

He thought about how he would question her and began to whistle as he walked.

CHAPTER 5

"You need a break." Nick set a cup of black coffee in front of Selena. Steam rose from the surface. "You've been sitting in that chair for hours."

Selena's desk was littered with notes and references. She leaned back, stretching.

"Thanks." She picked up the coffee, blew on it and took a sip.

"Did you learn anything new?"

"The pillar was erected during the reign of King Menes, which makes it more than five thousand years old. What I've translated so far falls right in line with legends about Atlantis. Sometimes legends are all that's left when history has disappeared."

"How is the inscription like the legends?"

"It describes a city built on a plain with a mountain in the center. It has three concentric rings marked off by canals, with the ruler's palace in the central ring. That fits with Plato's description."

"You really think this is about Atlantis." It wasn't a question.

"It's beginning to look that way."

"What did Plato say?"

"The first known mention of Atlantis comes in two of his dialogues, *Timaeus* and *Critia*. According to Plato, Athens is supposed to have defeated Atlantis in a great naval battle. There's no historical record of a battle like that ever taking place."

"Why write about it if it never happened?"

"His dialogues are mostly political allegory meant to glorify the Athenian way of life. There have always been people who think Atlantis was real. They argue Plato was using an historical example that the people of his time would have recognized. A historian named Crantor was a contemporary of Plato. He claimed to have interviewed Egyptian priests who showed him the history of Atlantis written down on pillars. The pillar in the photograph could be one of those."

"That's a pretty big stretch."

"It fits, doesn't it?"

"It still doesn't prove Atlantis was real."

"No, but what if it was? What if this inscription is referring to a source of power that could be re-discovered and used? It would benefit everyone."

"Or it could be turned into a weapon," Nick said. "That would be another reason for the Russians to go after Sokolov."

"The implications of this are endless," Selena said. "Take the pyramids, for example. Archaeologists still argue about how the Egyptians built them using those huge blocks of stone. Some of them weigh hundreds of tons and they're fitted together with perfection. How did they get them into place? If the inscription describes something real, it explains how it was done."

"I thought they dragged them behind slaves and built ramps as they went up. Like in the movies."

"Maybe for the lower levels, but there's a point where that can't be done anymore." Selena tapped her notes with her finger. "One of the theories is that the pyramid builders had something like what's described on this pillar and used it to to lift the stones through the air. Antigravity, if you like."

"Next you're going to tell me aliens did it."

"The UFO people would probably say something like that but you don't need aliens if this inscription is accurate."

Nick shook his head. "I've never seen anything that backs up the idea the pyramids were built by people from Atlantis. There isn't any proof Atlantis ever existed."

"This photograph could be the proof. Besides, no one is quite sure how old the pyramids are. Some archaeologists think the pyramids and the Sphinx are a lot older than they're supposed to be."

"How much older?"

"Most think the great pyramid was built about 2560 BCE. The Sphinx is supposed to be from around the same time. But there are experts who insist there's enough evidence to date the Sphinx as early as 10,000 BCE or earlier. The face of the Pharaoh may have been carved out at a later date."

"That's impossible."

"Not if the Sphinx was placed there by an earlier civilization. There's an account from the time of Khufu that says it was buried up to its neck in sand when it was discovered. Khufu is supposed to have built the great pyramid."

"Without more than this photograph there's no way to verify any of this," Nick said.

"That's why we need to go look for that pillar. There might be something in the rest of this inscription that could do that."

"And if there isn't?"

"We still have the map."

"You want to look for more records in Egypt?"

"It might be the only way to prove this one way or the other."

Selena sipped her coffee.

"I was thinking about the Russians. If they caught up with Sokolov, they'll know he sent the picture and the map to me. They might want them back."

"The thought had occurred to me." Nick sighed. "If they're serious, they'll come looking for it."

3

"I'll say one thing. Things haven't been dull since the first day we met."

Nick laughed. "That's not a day we're likely to forget."

"I don't ever want to have another day like that one." Selena picked up the photograph. "Something's bothering me about this. I think I've seen this writing before, but I can't remember where."

"It will come back to you."

"Or not. I'd better get back to work."

"I'm going for a run," Nick said. "There's still plenty of light."

Selena turned back to her study of the inscription on the pillar. Vaguely, she registered the door closing behind him as he left.

An hour later, she finished translating a long passage.

Wait until Elizabeth hears this.

CHAPTER 6

Nick and Selena were in Elizabeth's office.

"A stone?" Elizabeth said. "They used a stone to move things?"

"It could be some kind of crystal. Maybe a meteorite. I can't tell from what I've seen so far. They called it the Stone of the Gods."

"Selena, I have to ask you this. Please don't take it the wrong way."

Selena waited.

"Have you been taking drugs? A new prescription, perhaps?"

Selena snorted. "No, Elizabeth, no drugs. No funny cigarettes or anything else. I can't help it if this sounds like something out of an opium dream."

"The whole thing is fantastic," Elizabeth said.

"There's more. The inscription mentions an underground archive where all the knowledge of Atlantis was stored for safekeeping."

"An underground archive?" Elizabeth looked at Selena, astonished. "Are you sure?"

"An archive or a library. "

"Where was it located?"

"All I know is that it's underground and that it's guarded. That could mean anything. If we could find it, it would be the greatest archaeological discovery ever made. Nothing else even comes close."

"Wouldn't it have been lost in whatever disaster destroyed Atlantis? Assuming this really is about Atlantis in the first place."

"The hieroglyphic part of the inscription says that '*in the days before the great King Menes*' Atlantis conquered what is now Egypt and Libya. King Menes ruled five thousand years ago. The pillar was found in Egypt. If the archive wasn't in Atlantis it might be in one of those two countries. There could be records about this stone they used to produce power."

"If the records exist."

Selena nodded. "If they exist and if we can find them."

Elizabeth tapped her fingers on her desk. "Those are two big ifs."

"The Russians will translate the inscription. When they do, they'll start looking for that archive. I've translated what can be seen on the column and the location isn't there. No one is going to find anything without more information."

"When are Ronnie and Lamont coming back, Director?" Nick asked. "I thought they'd be here today."

"Ronnie has one more follow-up test this morning. Lamont is coming in this afternoon. He's cleared for light duty only. I'm going to put him in the armory for now. We've got the new MP-7s to familiarize ourselves with."

Nick grunted. "About time we got those. It seems like all the bad guys wear armor these days. Our MP-5s don't cut it anymore."

"Schedule weapons practice with Lamont. Once you're comfortable with the guns on the range, take everyone through the combat target course and see how they do."

The combat target course was set up in a warehouse-like
building across from Project Headquarters. It could be
configured as a town, city or country environment. As a
shooter went through the course, life-size targets popped out
at unexpected times from unexpected places. Some were bad
guys, others were noncombatant civilians. Deciding which
was which had to be done in a fraction of a second. Grading
was based on speed, hits and accurate choices. Shooting an
assailant aiming a weapon was good. Shooting a civilian
carrying a baby was not so good. It was easy to make a
mistake when it counted for real.

"Who gets to set up the course?" Nick asked.

"Lamont, of course."

"That should make it interesting."

Selena stirred in her seat. "I was telling Nick I thought I'd
seen something similar to that inscription."

"Where?" Elizabeth asked.

"I just remembered while we were talking. I read an article
a few months ago about the French Museum of Natural
History. They were in the midst of a major renovation and
discovered a disused storeroom in the basement. It was filled
with broken furniture and the like. There was a photograph of
the room in the article. I'm sure I saw something in the picture
with writing similar to what's on the column."

"Wouldn't the museum put it on display?" Elizabeth
asked.

"Not necessarily. They have more than enough artifacts.
One more or less doesn't make any difference, unless it's
historically important. They might not even have tried to
translate it."

"Can you find that article with the photograph?"

"I think so."

"Go look for it."

"If it's where I think it is, I can lay my hands on it and be
back here in a couple of hours."

"Good. Nick, while she's doing that why don't you start with the guns? Everything's down there ready to be unpacked."

"Shouldn't I wait for Lamont?"

"He won't mind if you open up a couple of crates and get a head start."

Ten minutes later Selena had gone back to their loft and Nick was down in the armory prying open a crate containing the Heckler and Koch MP-7 submachine guns. They'd been shipped wrapped in a polyester film called boPET. It beat the old days, when weapons were often covered in a thick coat of cosmoline that took hours to remove. He took out one of the guns and stripped away the protective covering.

The MP-7 had been purpose-designed to defeat an enemy wearing body armor. It took a specialized 4.6 X 30 mm cartridge unique to the gun. The round could punch through twenty layers of Kevlar. A 9mm or a .45 couldn't do that. A .45 slug would hurt like hell and knock the bad guy down but he could get up again and keep shooting.

The gun had all the bells and whistles German engineering could think of: an extendable stock and folding fore grip, a Picatinny rail to handle various accessories, places to attach optical sites and lasers, folding iron sights and a magazine capacity up to forty rounds. It was small enough to use like a pistol but easily turned into a full-fledged assault weapon.

The compact, lethal package weighed in at a little over four pounds.

Someone's always coming up with better ways for you to kill people.

The thought took Nick by surprise. It made him uneasy. He wasn't given to introspection on the firing range. He looked down at the precision weapon in his hands, an instrument of death.

You and the Grim Reaper, buddy, his inner voice said.

He set the gun down on the table. His hands were sweating.

Maybe it's time for me to quit, he thought.

CHAPTER 7

Selena had found the magazine with the article about the French museum. Now she was back at Project Headquarters, showing the picture she'd remembered to Elizabeth and Nick.

"You can make out the corner of a stone tablet behind that pile of broken chairs. The picture is blurry but you can see some writing on it. It's the same script as in the photograph."

"I guess we're going to Paris," Nick said.

"It's the only way to see what's on that tablet."

"How are you going to persuade them to show it to you?"

"I don't think it will be difficult," Selena said. "My reputation will get me in the door."

"You'll have to go commercial," Elizabeth said. "The Gulfstream is down for maintenance."

"I checked the schedules. There's a flight to Paris from Dulles leaving at six tonight."

"What about our weapons?" Nick said.

"You know the French are touchy about that. Even if you box them for the plane there's no guarantee you'll get them back after you land. You shouldn't need them."

"I've heard that too many times to put much faith in it."

Selena said, "It should be all right. We'll only be there long enough to photograph the tablet and go back to the airport for the flight home."

That evening they boarded an Air France flight to Paris and settled into business class. The seats were wide and comfortable. Once they were in the air Nick ordered an Irish whiskey. Selena asked for a mimosa.

Nick sampled his drink and leaned back.

"Sometimes I wish the only language you understood was English."

"If that were the case we wouldn't get to go to all these interesting places."

"Yeah, like Mali and Algeria. Or Pakistan. Real tourist spots."

"It's not always like that. Tomorrow will be interesting. You'll see."

Nick dozed in fits and starts on the plane. His dreams were jumbled, unpleasant. The next morning they had breakfast at a sidewalk café and took a cab to the French National Museum of Natural History.

The museum was situated in the heart of Paris on the left bank of the Seine in the *Jardin des Plantes*, once the Royal botanical garden. The neoclassical building dominated the landscape.

"Big, isn't it?" Nick said.

"This is only one location. There are fourteen sites, four of them here in Paris. This is the original and the most impressive. Wait until you see the Grand Gallery."

"You've been here before?"

"The first time was when I was a child. My uncle brought me here when I was eleven."

Selena had called ahead and arranged to see the tablet in the basement. As she'd predicted, her credentials had smoothed the way. They were met by the assistant director of the museum, Pierre Arnaud. Arnaud was dressed in a French suit with broad pinstripes that made him look like a gangster from a black and white movie. Nick could almost hear Edith Piaf singing in the background.

In spite of his suit, Arnaud wasn't a bad looking man. He affected a thin mustache that reinforced the retro look. He greeted Selena in a stream of French and kissed her on both cheeks, as if she were a long lost friend.

Selena responded in fluent French and introduced Nick. The assistant director's handshake was polite. Selena and Arnaud started down the hall, chatting away in French. Nick followed along, wondering what they were talking about.

At the entrance to the storeroom, Arnaud seemed to realize Nick was there and switched to English.

"Please excuse the clutter, Doctor Connor. We have many priorities and this room has not been one of them. It's full of discarded items, mostly junk. Your phone call reminded me that it's time we sorted it out. I had one of the custodians clear away a path to the tablet that interests you."

"There's no need to apologize, Monsieur Arnaud. I am curious, though. An artifact like this seems out of place in a natural history museum. How did it come to be here?"

"Ah, that is an interesting story. You are familiar with Bonaparte's campaign in Egypt?"

"Only in the broadest sense. It was never a field of study for me."

"Bonaparte's Army was accompanied by the great natural historian Gregory Saint-Hilaire. His task during the campaign was to collect and catalog specimens as the Army moved through Egypt. Most of his collection involved native flora and fauna, as well as fossilized relics and various kinds of Egyptian artifacts from the tombs and elsewhere. I know you are familiar with the Rosetta Stone. Did you know it was found by a French corporal during the campaign?"

"I did," Selena said. "The stone takes its name from a nearby town."

"*Oui.* When Napoleon abandoned Egypt he left his army behind. The British surrounded them at Alexandria and forced a surrender. The British commander was determined to steal everything Saint-Hilaire had collected but in the end, a negotiation was made. The British took the Rosetta Stone and Saint-Hilaire kept almost everything else he had collected, including this tablet you are about to see."

"Where was it found?" Selena asked.

"Close to Libya, in a temple near the Egyptian coast. It's odd that it was placed down here. There's no record of why it was stored in this room or how Saint-Hilaire got it past the British."

"It does seem like they'd want to keep it," Selena said.

Arnaud took out a set of keys and opened the door. He held it back for Selena and Nick to enter. As he'd warned, the room was a hodgepodge of things piled and stacked in no particular order. The tablet stood against the far wall, at the end of a narrow aisle cleared through the junk.

It was covered from top to bottom with script in the same language as the writing on the Egyptian column in the Russian photograph. Selena took one look and smiled. Even Nick could see the similarity.

"What do you think?" Nick asked.

"It's wonderful. It will take some time to translate but I can't wait to find out what it says."

She turned to Arnaud. "With your permission, I'd like to photograph the tablet. When I've completed the translation I'll be happy to send it to you."

"That is acceptable." Arnaud looked at her. "What exactly is your interest in this particular artifact?"

Selena wasn't about to tell him it might be the key to unraveling the legend of Atlantis.

"It's assumed the Minoans traded with Egypt but no one has ever found anything there with their writing on it. This tablet may be historical proof of Minoan interaction with ancient Egypt. It could shed new light on the Minoan civilization and the Egyptian world of that time."

The explanation seemed to satisfy Arnaud. "How did you learn of it?"

"An article about the ongoing renovations of the museum. There was a picture of this room."

"Fascinating."

Selena took a camera from a small pack she carried at her waist and began taking pictures. She stepped closer and tripped over a piece of wood lying on the floor. She put her hand out against the stone tablet to break her fall.

The tablet moved.

"How did you do that?" Nick said. "That thing has to weigh a thousand pounds."

Selena looked mystified. "I don't know." She turned to Arnaud. "Has anyone tried to move this?"

I don't think so. There wasn't any reason to. Besides, it appears to weigh quite a bit. I would assume it will need equipment or several very strong men to move it."

"Let's see," Nick said.

He went to the tablet and grasped it on both sides. He grunted once and shifted it two inches to the right.

"You must have been taking your vitamins," Selena said.

"It looks a lot heavier than it is. I wonder what kind of stone was used?"

Arnaud was suddenly energized. "This makes it of great interest to us. A new, undiscovered mineral would be a scientific discovery of the first rank."

"That could be why the guy who found it hid it away," Nick said. "He probably wanted the glory of a new discovery for himself."

Arnaud looked offended. "Saint-Hilaire was one of the luminaries of French science. I'm sure his actions were taken for the purest of reasons. His reputation is beyond reproach."

Selena stopped Nick from saying anything else with a light touch on his arm.

"I'm sure that's true, Monsieur Arnaud. Everyone is aware of the great contributions France has made to human knowledge. Your museum is a testament to that quest."

Nick looked at the ceiling.

Arnaud said, "Well. We will certainly examine the tablet more closely. Have you got all the pictures you need?"

"I do, thank you."

Nick looked at his watch. "We have time to make the afternoon flight if we leave now."

Selena smiled at Arnaud. "Thank you so much, Monsieur Arnaud. You have been very helpful. As soon as I have completed my translation I will send you a full report."

"My pleasure. In the meantime, we'll begin working on a translation here."

"Then we'll be able to compare notes," Selena said.

During the brief exchange they'd moved out into the hall.

"I need to talk to the custodians about this room," Arnaud said. "Do you think you can find your way back to the entrance? If you take those stairs at the end of the hall, it will bring you out near the main gallery."

"Of course. Thank you again for your hospitality." Selena smiled at him.

As they climbed the stairs Nick said, "You laid it on a little thick in there."

"You insulted him when you said Saint-Hilaire acted out of personal motives."

"Why are the French so prickly? They always seem to take offense at nothing."

"I'm not sure. I don't think they ever quite got over the loss of their empire under Napoleon."

"Hell, that was more than two hundred years ago."

"The world's center of power has shifted a long way from Paris. Pride is a hard thing to let go of."

"My mother used to say pride and a dollar will get you on the bus."

"It takes more than a dollar these days," Selena said.

CHAPTER 8

Three men sat in a car parked in front of an office building near Dupont Circle.

"This isn't somebody's home."

The speaker was Vasily Ivanov, one of the two men Borya Yeltsin had brought with him to America. The driver was named Viktor. Both were seasoned Spetsnaz veterans.

Yeltsin looked at him. "Really? Your powers of observation astound me. This is the address where Sokolov sent the map and photograph. Wait here. I want to see who works in that building."

He got out of the car, strolled over to the building and pushed through the glass doors. A security guard sat behind a counter at the back wall across from the entrance, reading a paper. He barely looked up as Yeltsin entered. A directory near the doors listed the building's occupants. Yeltsin scanned the list, looking for something to tell him where Sokolov's letter had ended up. He'd expected to find a residence, not an office building.

"Can I help you?" the guard called across the lobby.

"No thank you." Yeltsin's English was perfect. "I think I have the wrong building."

Yeltsin had an eidetic memory. One glance at the list was enough to imprint it firmly in his mind. He went back outside and got into the car.

"Well?" Vasily asked.

"Quiet. Let me think for a moment."

What stood out on the list? There had been several lawyers. If the letter had gone to one of them, it was going to be difficult to discover which was the correct target. A business consulting firm was listed but that didn't seem to fit. The top floor of the building was given over to an entertainment and booking agency.

"Go back to the hotel," Yeltsin said.

Back in his room, Yeltsin got out a laptop computer and began researching the names and firms on the list. It didn't take long to find what he was looking for.

"Clever old bastard."

"Major?" Viktor was confused.

"Sokolov sent the letter to a booking agency that handles entertainers and speakers. The woman probably uses the agency as a cut out to keep her address private."

"Why would she use a booking agency?"

"Because she is a well-known lecturer," Yeltsin said.

He turned the computer toward Viktor. Selena's picture and academic resumé showed on the screen.

"Her specialty is extinct languages. It explains why Sokolov would send the picture to her. He would want to know about the parts of the inscription he couldn't understand. He thought she'd be able to translate it"

"What do you want to do?" Vasily asked.

"Tonight we come back. The woman's address will be in a file in that office. Once we have that, the rest is simple."

Late in the evening of the same day, Michael Daly was still at his desk. Daly owned the booking agency that handled Selena's professional correspondence. At the moment, he was thinking that being the boss of a successful company wasn't always what it was cracked up to be. Today he'd had to soothe the egos of a B-list male film actor, cancel the next tour stop for a troupe of Mexican acrobats and placate an annoying Harvard professor. He was checking the final details for the acrobats' new itinerary when he heard the elevator stop at his floor.

Who the hell is that at this time of night? he thought. *How did they get past the security desk?*

He picked up his phone and called downstairs. Security didn't answer, which was odd. Daly was a veteran of Afghanistan. All at once he felt the odd sensation at the base of his skull that warned of danger. He hadn't had that feeling for a long time, not since Helmland Province. It made him wish he had a gun.

The District of Columbia had rigid gun laws that made it impossible to get a carry permit. Inside the Beltway nobody had guns except the bad guys and the cops. Daly had a pistol at home in his Alexandria apartment, but it wasn't much good to him at the moment.

This is foolish. Nobody's coming in that door with an AK or a grenade. Get hold of yourself.

That was when Yeltsin came through the door, a Makarov 10 mm pistol in his hand. Daly's mind went into overdrive.

shit what can I use I need a weapon he's got a suppressor on that piece three is too many

"Who the hell are you?"

"Be quiet," Yeltsin said. "Put your hands on top of the desk where I can see them. Cooperate, and you won't be hurt."

"What do you want? There's no cash here."

Viktor and Vasily moved to stand on each side of Daly's chair.

"I don't want cash," Yeltsin said. "Only information. Put your hands on the desk."

Yeltsin gestured with the pistol. Daly put his hands out on the desk.

"Okay. What information?"

"You received a package from Amsterdam recently. Don't lie. I can see you did in your eyes."

"No. I never received such a package."

"Viktor," Yeltsin said.

For a big man, Viktor moved with the swiftness of a striking snake. He grabbed the back of Daly's head and drove it face down into the hard wooden surface of the desk. There was the dull crack of cartilage breaking.

Viktor pulled him back up by the hair. Blood streamed down Daly's face. His nose was smashed, pushed to the side.

"I told you not to lie. Did you receive the package?"

"Yes, damn it."

"See? All you had to do was tell the truth. Where is it now?"

"I don't have it."

"Viktor..."

"Wait," Daly said. "It was addressed to someone else. I forwarded it."

As soon as he said it, he wished he hadn't. The pain of his broken nose made it hard to think. There was a brass lamp with a heavy base and sharp corners on the desk, not far from his left hand. He ran a scenario through his mind.

Grab the lamp. Smash the guy on the left with a backhand to the head. Drop behind the desk and take the second guy down at the knee. He's gotta be armed. Get his weapon.

It was a stretch, but he couldn't think of anything else to do. He was damned if he was going to knuckle under to them. Besides, they didn't have the look of men who would leave him alive when they left.

Nothing to lose.

"Yes, I got a package. I don't know what was in it."

"You sent it to someone?"

"Yes, to a client."

"That client would be a woman named Connor?"

Daly made his move. He grabbed the lamp and brought it around in an arc and slammed it into the side of Viktor's skull. The big man grunted and went down. Daly pivoted toward the second man, aiming for his left knee.

Yeltsin's first shot took Daly under his arm. The second one blew out the side of his head. The body fell sideways to the floor.

"Shit," Vasily said.

Yeltsin put away the Makarov. "I'm going to look at the files on his computer. Help Viktor."

"He doesn't look so good."

"Do what you can."

Yeltsin began searching Daly's files on his computer. He scrolled through the directory until he found a folder labeled *Current Clients*. He opened the folder and looked for Selena's name. It only took seconds to locate it. He memorized her address.

Viktor was conscious. He sat up, holding his head.

"Bastard got me good."

Yeltsin went over to where Viktor sat on the floor.

"Vasily, help me get him up."

The two men got Viktor onto his feet.

"Can you walk?"

"Da."

The three Russians closed the door behind them as they left.

CHAPTER 9

The next morning Volkov's men waited outside the building of converted lofts where Nick and Selena lived. The target was inside with her husband. The Russians were waiting for them to leave.

Viktor lit a cigarette. The side of his face was purple and bruised.

"It's a soft target. Getting in will be easy."

Vasily coughed. "Do you have to smoke inside the car?"

"I like American cigarettes."

"At least roll down the window."

Viktor muttered under his breath and lowered the window partway. He looked in the rearview mirror at Vasily in the back seat.

"What did you say?"

"Nothing."

"I didn't think so," Vasily said.

"Stop this bickering," Yeltsin said. He sat up straight in his seat. "There she is. In the green Mercedes."

Selena's Mercedes emerged from the underground parking garage and turned right onto the street.

"We give them a few minutes, then go in," Yeltsin said. "The woman is rich. There might be servants. If there are, act as though it's a robbery."

"The Americans must pay their spies well," Vasily said.

"Idiot. She inherited the money," Yeltsin said.

He looked at his watch. "It's been long enough. Let's go. Drive into the parking garage. There'll be an elevator or stairs."

They drove into the underground garage and parked. The elevator was at the far end. There were only a few cars, leaving most of the garage empty. The target lived on the top floor. Yeltsin pushed the button and the doors opened.

"You need a key for each floor," Viktor said.

"It's not a problem," Yeltsin said. "Remember your training."

He took a small leather pouch from his pocket, opened it and extracted two tools from a set of lock picks. It took seconds to turn the lock. He punched the button.

They rode the elevator to the top floor and stepped out into an entrance foyer about twenty feet square. The floor was of polished oak, the walls painted a soothing peach color. A pair of framed watercolors decorated the space. The door to the loft was opposite the elevator on the other side of the foyer. There were two locks on it. A discrete camera peered at them from over the door.

"She has the entire floor?" Vasily asked.

"I told you, she's rich. Her husband is also a spy. She's the one with the money."

Yeltsin manipulated his picks. After a minute the first lock clicked.

"This is high-end stuff," he said.

He worked with the picks until he could open the door. The three men entered the loft. An alarm blinked yellow on the wall next to the door. A digital clock counted down seconds until the alarm would sound. There was a camera farther along the wall. A steady red light showed it was powered on. Yeltsin took out a small, electric screwdriver and had the cover off the box in seconds. He took a device from his other pocket and hooked two wires to terminals inside the box and twisted a dial. The counter stopped with three seconds to go. The light on the camera died.

Vasily looked around the loft and whistled.

"All this space for two people?" He walked over to the wall of windows facing the Potomac and Virginia. "Look at that view."

"Were not here to sightsee. Start looking for the map. Try not to mess everything up. We don't want them to know we were here. Vasily, take the bedrooms. Viktor, you take those rooms on the right. I'll start with the living area."

An hour and a half later they were still looking.

Viktor called from the room he was searching.

"I found a safe."

Yeltsin and Vasily joined him. Viktor had turned back a Persian rug, revealing a safe with a combination dial set into the floor.

"You don't see these much anymore," Vasily said. "Everything's digital and biometric now."

"A combination lock is a better bet. Safer," Yeltsin said. "Electronic locks and biometric readers fail, even the good ones. With a combination, you can always get it open."

"Can you open it?"

"Of course I can. It may take some time. Find a glass. A wine glass, with a stem."

Vasily went to the kitchen and came back with a glass. Yeltsin knelt by the safe and placed the glass upside down on the door. He laid his left ear on the thin base and began to turn the dial with his right hand.

That was when Selena came home.

CHAPTER 10

Selena had come back for some notes she'd forgotten. The first sign something was wrong was the elevator in the garage. The light behind the button for her floor was lit, waiting for someone to push it.

It should have been off.

She eased her pistol from its holster as the elevator rose. She carried a SIG-Sauer 229 chambered for .40 Smith & Wesson. She liked the shorter barrel and lower weight of the 229, plus it came out of the holster a little bit faster. At the distance where personal shootouts happened, the extra barrel length of the 226 favored by many in the specialized services didn't make any difference. She could empty a magazine into the center mass of a target with either one.

The gun was fully loaded, a round in the chamber. Selena eased the hammer back and laid her finger alongside the trigger guard.

The elevator opened onto the empty foyer. The door to the loft was ajar. She thought about calling Nick but discarded the idea as quickly as it came. The noise would give her away if someone was inside. If no one was there, so much the better. If they were, they weren't going to violate her personal space without paying for it.

Whoever it was, they were good. Getting through the locks was the least of it. Somehow they'd managed to turn off the alarm.

With a gentle push, she eased the door partway open. She heard voices.

Russian. They're speaking Russian.

Her heart began pounding as adrenaline flooded her. She took a deep breath and listened to what they were saying.

They found the safe.

She pushed her shoes off in the foyer and slipped through the door. Her feet made no sound as she padded across the floor. She moved to the wall and worked her way along it until she was outside the entrance to her study.

"I have three numbers," someone said. "One more and I'll have it open."

"We've been here a long time," someone else said. "Can't you hurry it up, Major?"

At least two, she thought.

"Don't bother him, Vasily. You wouldn't have gotten through those locks on the door."

Three.

"What if they come back?"

"They went to work. They're not coming back. If they do, we take care of it."

"Will you two shut up? How can I hear what I'm doing with your yammering?"

Selena heard the click as the last tumbler fell into place, then the metallic ratcheting of the handle that pulled back the locking bars inside the safe door.

"It's open," the first voice said.

"Is the map in there?" The second voice said.

"I don't see it."

Time to introduce myself, Selena thought.

She was angry. These thugs had come into her home, into her private space. She stepped into the room with her pistol held in front of her in both hands. One man knelt over the open safe. The other two stood nearby.

"Don't fucking move," she said in Russian.

Yeltsin looked up from the floor and saw an angry woman with intense violet eyes, holding an automatic pistol pointed at him. Without thinking he reached for his Makarov.

Selena's first shot sounded like a cannon in the confines of the room. It hit Yeltsin and bowled him over. She shifted to the right and shot Vasily, two rounds into his chest. He staggered and fell onto his back, knocking over a floor lamp as he went down. She swiveled toward the third man. He was trying to free his gun from his pocket. He grabbed a book from her desk and hurled it at her. The book struck her hand as she fired. The round missed. The slide locked halfway back and stopped.

Jammed!

She didn't have time to think about it. Viktor charged her. He was a big man, fast for his size. She threw her gun at him. It bounced off his shoulder. He barreled into her and knocked her down. As she fell she swept her leg around and took his foot out from under him. He went to the floor, cursing. She arched and flipped backward onto her feet. Viktor reached out and grabbed her ankle and pulled. She twisted and felt a jolt of pain as she went down. She fell on top of him and drove her thumb into his eye.

He screamed and grasped at her. She brought her elbow down hard on his face and heard bone break under the blow. She slammed his throat with her elbow, once, twice, and rolled away. He thrashed on the floor trying to breathe.

The first man she'd shot lifted his pistol. She rolled to the side as he fired. Hot, electric pain shot up her leg from the injured ankle. The barrel of the Makarov was aimed straight at her.

No.

The pistol wavered. Yeltsin coughed. Bright red blood vomited from his mouth. He collapsed and lay still. His bowels let go and a sewer stench filled the room. Selena gagged.

Shaken, she crawled to the desk and pulled herself up on her good leg. She tried to put weight on the injured foot and felt the warning pain. She looked at the bodies of the men she'd killed. The clock on her desk showed a few minutes after ten in the morning.

Hell of a way to start the day, she thought.

She picked up the phone and called Elizabeth.

A cleanup team arrived at the loft less than half an hour after she'd called. Nick showed up ten minutes later.

"You're all right?"

"Yes. I hurt my ankle when that asshole grabbed it." She gestured at Viktor's body. "I can't put any weight on it."

"Stinks in here. Come on, let's get out while the cleaners finish up. Lean on my arm," Nick said.

"It's a good thing there's no one on the floor below us," Selena said. "No one heard the shots."

She hobbled with him over to the elevator. They descended to the parking garage.

"Wait here."

Nick got the car and brought it over. He opened the door and Selena dropped into the passenger seat.

It wasn't until they'd crossed over into Virginia that she began shaking.

Nick pulled over to the side of the highway. He took off his jacket and placed it around her shoulders.

"You're okay," he said.

"I know." She wrapped her arms around herself. "One of them was pointing his pistol at me. I couldn't get out of the way. I couldn't do anything. I thought I was going to die."

"But you didn't."

"Not this time."

"Not next time, either."

"I don't know if I believe that anymore," Selena said.

"You have to believe it. So do I. If we don't believe it, we can't do what we do."

They spent the rest of the ride in silence.

CHAPTER 11

"Thank God you're okay," Elizabeth said.

Lamont, Ronnie and Stephanie were in the room. Lamont had probed at Selena's injury and taped her ankle and foot.

"You sprained it pretty bad," he said, "maybe tore a ligament. There's no way to tell without an MRI. Keep it taped up and try not to get in any more fights."

He grinned at her.

She looked down at her foot, wrapped in white tape. "Thanks. Where did you learn how to do that? I think I'll start calling you Doc."

"You learn a lot of stuff like that in the SEALS."

"It's good to see you back."

"It's good to be here."

Lamont had been in the hospital for weeks, then rehab after that. Two shots to the chest had almost killed him. He was thinner than his usual wiry self. His rich, coffee-colored skin looked washed out. Selena thought his blue eyes seemed brighter than they had before but told herself she was imagining it.

Ronnie looked at what Lamont had done and nodded approval.

"Not bad for a swabbie," he said.

"Coming from a jarhead like you, I suppose that's a compliment," Lamont said.

Elizabeth interrupted. "Ronnie, Lamont, now's not the time."

"Sorry, Director."

"We need to think about what happened." She turned to Selena. "You're positive they were Russian?"

"I'm certain. The one they addressed as major had a strong Moscow accent. You can't mistake it. They were after Sokolov's map."

Stephanie said, "Two of the bodies had Spetsnaz tattoos."

"They have to be FSB," Nick said.

"Or SVR," Ronnie said.

"Or GRU or MVD. All the Russian security forces have Spetsnaz personnel. My money's on the FSB. They're the ones who were after Sokolov."

"No matter who it was, the ante just went up," Elizabeth said. "The Russians know Selena works for us. They wanted that map badly enough to risk a confrontation on our home turf."

"Which they got." Nick scratched his ear.

"Didn't work out quite the way they expected," Lamont said.

"The cleanup team found Serbian passports on the bodies," Stephanie said.

"No way those men were Serbs," Selena said.

"I can work with the pictures on the passports. If they turn up in the database, I can identify them."

Elizabeth said, "That might help pin down who sent them, FSB or someone else."

"What are we going to do about it?" Nick asked. "This isn't business as usual. Maybe they were hoping to get the map without running into Selena, but they tried to kill her when she showed up."

"They might make another attempt," Elizabeth said.

"Would you?"

"I wouldn't try to steal it. There's no way they can get to it now. They know we'll be waiting for them."

"It wasn't in the loft anyway," Selena said. "What would they have done when they found out it wasn't there?"

"That's easy," Ronnie said. "You know what's on the map. I were them, I'd grab you and make you tell me what was on it."

"Thanks. I'll sleep a lot better tonight because of that."

"Hey, I'm just telling it like it is."

"He's right," Nick said. "If they can't get the map, Selena is the next best thing. They'll try again."

"Not those bozos," Lamont said. "They're not going anywhere."

"The Russians have plenty of bozos. They'll just send different ones."

Ronnie rubbed a hand across his close cropped hair. His face was thinner than before he'd been shot, though his Roman nose was as big as ever. He'd lost weight in the hospital, more when he'd gone home to the Navajo reservation. The doctors had patched up his body. The traditional rituals of his people had restored his spirit.

"Seems like a lot of effort for what might turn out to be a myth," he said.

Selena held up her phone with a picture of the French tablet.

"When I've translated this we'll know more."

Elizabeth asked, "When will you have it done?"

"I'm not sure. There's quite a bit here and I'm only beginning to get a grasp on it. Perhaps a few days?"

"How did they know where you lived?" Ronnie asked.

Selena looked stricken. "I hadn't thought of that. That letter was sent to my agent. I'd better call him."

She took out her phone and dialed. An unfamiliar male voice answered.

"Detective D'Angelo."

"You're the police? Is Michael Daly there?"

Elizabeth raised an eyebrow.

"Who's calling?"

"A friend. Would you put Mike on please?"

"Give me your name and number and I'll have him call you back."

"Has something happened?" She heard people talking in the background.

"There's been an accident," D'Angelo said. "I can't tell you more than that right now. Give me your name and number and we'll call back."

Selena hung up the phone.

"A detective answered the phone. The cops are there and I could hear people in the background."

"What did he say?" Nick asked.

"He said there'd been an accident. He wanted my name and number and said he'd call me back. I didn't think it was a good idea to give it to him."

"That was the right choice," Elizabeth said. "The last thing we need is to get mixed up with the police on this."

"Mike was in Afghanistan, a Ranger. He was a combat vet. He wouldn't have given them my address without a fight."

"He might be okay," Nick said.

"You know he isn't," she said. Her voice was bitter. "Why else would the cops be there?"

Elizabeth cleared her throat.

"I'll find out what happened. In the meantime you all have something to do. Selena, your priority is the translation of the tablet. Nick, you and Ronnie work with the new guns. Lamont, set up the combat course. See if you can add a few new twists. When Selena's done with the translation, get her up to speed on the MP-7 and then take everyone through the course. Steph, track down those thugs. Let's find out who sent them."

Later, they would look back on that day as the beginning.

CHAPTER 12

On the top floor of the SVR headquarters building in Moscow, General Alexei Vysotsky put down the report from Washington. He took a deep breath to calm his rising blood pressure. Three FSB agents, dead in the home of two of Harker's operatives. Volkov had poked a stick into a hornet's nest.

That meddling bastard has done it now. What the hell was he thinking?

It was late in the afternoon. Outside Vysotsky's window, a sea of leafy green treetops stretched all the way to the Moscow river flowing past the walls of the Kremlin. It was the best time of year in the city, when the arctic cold of winter was gone and the brutal heat of summer had not yet arrived. Most of the time in Russia it was too hot or too cold.

Vysotsky set the report down and opened the left-hand bottom drawer in his desk. He took out a bottle of vodka and a tumbler, filled the eight ounce glass and drank half of it down. Vysotsky considered vodka a good replacement for water. He couldn't drink as much as when he was young but he could still hold his own with the best of them. As long as he didn't overdo it, vodka helped him think when he was confronted with an annoying problem.

Like Volkov.

Volkov was doing everything he could to curry favor with Vladimir Orlov. He wanted the Federation president to think Alexei was unfit to run Russia's powerful foreign intelligence service and never missed a chance to undermine Vysotsky and SVR. Alexei suspected him of sabotaging two operations that had gone bad but couldn't prove it. Volkov wanted to establish a new KGB, with himself as Director. It wasn't hard for Alexei to imagine Volkov's motivation. It was exactly what he wanted for himself.

Vysotsky was certain Orlov saw through Volkov's manipulations, using them to keep the two intelligence agencies at odds. The oldest trick in the Russian political book was to divide and control.

Now Volkov had stepped over the line. He'd sent people to break into the home of an active American intelligence operative. Worse, he'd involved Elizabeth Harker's Project.

Besides, Alexei thought, *if anyone is going to do any breaking and entering in America it's going to be on my orders, not his.*

Why had Volkov done it? It was the last straw. It was time to do something about him but it wasn't going to be easy. He needed to pry Volkov out of Orlov's favor.

Alexei set the half empty glass of vodka down and closed his eyes, letting himself slip into a light meditative state where thoughts and bits of information mixed without interference. Vysotsky's mind was highly visual. He'd learned to trust the random association of images and ideas that surfaced during these sessions with himself.

The tension in his muscles eased as he relaxed. Images and thoughts began to flow.

The report from Washington... The face of Selena Connor... Elizabeth Harker's green eyes... Volkov, unsmiling... A report from an informant... FSB activity in Holland... A Russian archaeologist murdered in Amsterdam...

Alexei's eyes snapped open. He had spies planted throughout the ranks of the FSB. A week before, one of them had reported that Volkov was sending agents to Amsterdam. The informant hadn't known why.

A few days later a routine report from the SVR residency in Holland noted the death of Yuri Sokolov, an academic researcher from the Russian Academy of Sciences in Moscow. He'd been identified as a man found beaten to death three days earlier in his hotel room. There was no indication in the report of who had done it or why, or what Sokolov was doing in Amsterdam in the first place.

Until this moment, Alexei hadn't put the two pieces of information together.

It can't be coincidence. Volkov's men killed him. Why?

Vysotsky decided to find out.

CHAPTER 13

Selena rubbed her tired eyes. The pictures she'd taken of the tablet were displayed on her computer monitor, where she could zoom in on parts of the inscription with ease. She'd been at it for hours.

Some words had been easy, similar to the version of Linear A she was used to. Not that anything about Linear A was easy, even with the translation key she and Nick had discovered in Tibet. Selena had concluded that the stone was inscribed with a script predating Linear A. She'd decided to call it Linear D. There was already a Linear A, B and C. Linear C had been supplanted by early Greek.

Linear D taxed all of her considerable linguistic skills. Without the hieroglyphics inscribed on the Egyptian column, she wouldn't have gotten far. She could read and understand most of those. The hieroglyphics had helped her make sense of the Linear D on the pillar, but the pillar was only a warm-up for the French tablet.

Translation required much more than understanding symbols and words. The structure of the language was still confusing to her. It didn't help to know what a word meant if she couldn't put it in context with what went before or came after. Trying to understand the meaning of words without understanding how they related to each other was like listening to random radio signals from the universe, hoping to hear a message from another galaxy. The message might be there, but without comprehensible structure and context it was just static.

It was after two in the morning. She knew she'd get no more done tonight. The last time she'd seen Nick had been an hour ago when he'd looked in on her and told her he was going to bed. Selena yawned and decided he'd had the right idea. She turned out the light in the study and went into the master bedroom.

Nick lay naked on his back, the covers thrown onto the floor. He was making quick, erratic movements, muttering in his sleep. His body glistened with sweat.

He's having one of his nightmares, she thought. *They've come back since Germany.*

She was about to wake him when he shouted and sat up, sending a pillow flying.

"Nick. Wake up. It's all right, you're home."

She was careful to keep her distance. Sometimes he swung out wildly when he was having one of his dreams. Before they'd gotten married the nightmares had come close to driving them apart.

"Nick," she said again.

"What?" He opened his eyes, saw Selena standing nearby. "Oh."

"Afghanistan again?" she asked.

In Afghanistan Nick had almost been killed by a grenade thrown by a child. He'd shot the boy as the grenade was in the air. The boy's face haunted his worst dreams.

Nick rubbed his eyes. "Yeah. Only it was in Germany at the same time. In that café."

The café was where Ronnie and Lamont had been wounded. It had been a close call all around.

"Maybe you should make an appointment with Milton."

She meant the therapist Nick had seen a while back. Milton had served in Afghanistan and lost an arm to an IED. Nick respected him. He'd helped Nick work with the PTSD that sometimes froze him in place.

"Yeah. Maybe." He got out of bed. "I'm going to take a shower."

She watched him walk to the bathroom.

No point in going to bed now.

Selena was wide awake and Nick wouldn't go back to sleep tonight. She headed to the kitchen and turned on the lights, got out cups and started coffee. Nick would want some and she needed a jolt of energy.

It was while she waited for the coffee that the key to understanding the inscription on the tablet came to her. The coffee forgotten, she went back into her study, rebooted the computer and looked again at the pictures.

Yes! That's what I was missing.

Three hours later she'd finished the translation.

CHAPTER 15

Morning light streamed through the patio doors of Elizabeth's office. Ronnie and Lamont sat next to Nick and Selena on the couch in front of Elizabeth's desk. Stephanie took a seat nearby with her laptop.

Steph looks radiant, Selena thought. *I wonder if she's pregnant again?*

"I tracked down Sokolov," Stephanie said. "He's legitimate, regarded as a reliable researcher in Russian academic circles. He got in trouble once for speaking out against government restrictions on sharing research with academic colleagues in the West."

"Was he a political dissident?" Elizabeth asked.

"I suppose it's possible, but he still had his job at the Institute. He disappeared eight days ago. Selena said his letter was postmarked from Amsterdam. I searched through the newspapers from around the time it was mailed and found an article about an unidentified victim who was murdered in his hotel."

"You think it was Sokolov?" Elizabeth said.

"It fits. The man was tortured. It seems like too much of a coincidence."

Nick rubbed the back of his neck. "I knew it. If he was alive, he'd have shown up to talk with Selena."

Elizabeth picked up her pen and began tapping it on her desk. She caught herself and set it down.

"Selena, you look like the cat that ate the canary."

At the word cat, an enormous orange tomcat lying on the couch next to Selena looked up expectantly.

"No, Burps, it's not time for lunch."

Selena reached down and scratched the cat behind his ear, triggering a rumbling purr that vibrated under her touch.

"What I found will be challenged as a hoax. But I'm convinced that tablet is genuine and from Atlantis. No one could fake that language."

"Atlantis was real?" Lamont asked.

"If you believe what's on the tablet. It's a narrative of what the author calls the homeland. I think he was recording a contemporary history."

"I have a hard time believing any of this," Ronnie said.

"You're not the only one," Lamont said.

"Don't forget the pillar found in Egypt. That inscription fits with the stories about Atlantis."

"Still doesn't prove it." Ronnie crossed his arms over his chest.

"No, it doesn't. But what's on the Paris tablet ups the possibility. The scribe describes two different groups called the Sages and the Archons. He was in the first group."

"Sounds like something Hollywood would dream up," Lamont said.

"Give it a break, Lamont," Nick said. "Let her tell us the rest."

"Their government seems to have been a quasi-democratic monarchy. When the tablet was inscribed, the Archons were the dominant group. That's interesting because Archon is a Greek word for ruler or magistrate. Anyway, the two groups argued about how to use the power Sokolov talked about in his letter."

"What did they argue about?" Nick asked.

"The Archons wanted to create a weapon by increasing the power of the force they used to lift things. There's nothing on the tablet about why they wanted to do that or who they were going to use it against. The force was unstable. The Sages thought increasing the power would cause uncontrollable destruction. The Archons were determined to do it anyway."

"What happened?" Ronnie asked.

"The Sages couldn't stop what was happening. They built an archive to preserve the knowledge of the society in case something went wrong. That confirms what was written on the pillar in the photograph."

"And?" Elizabeth asked.

"The narrative ends there. It's incomplete."

"So we still don't know where this archive was."

"No."

"Then we're no better off than before."

"The Archons must have succeeded in what they were trying to do," Selena said.

"Why do you say that?"

"Something terrible happened to Atlantis. They were trying to build a weapon. I think they destroyed themselves with it."

"A weapon that got out of control," Nick said.

"Whatever that force was, it must've had enormous destructive power. There would be records of it in that archive. If there's any chance it still exists, we have to find it before the Russians do."

"Anything with that kind of possible weapons application has to be kept out of Russian hands," Elizabeth said. "Selena's right. We have to find that archive."

"Where do we begin looking?" Nick asked.

Selena brushed her hand across her forehead. "There could be another tablet with the location. Something that continues the narrative."

"The French tablet was discovered near the town of Marsá Matruh, the same place Sokolov mentions," Stephanie said. "I looked at satellite photos of the area. There are ruins of an Egyptian temple complex near there, right about where that mark is on the map. If there's another tablet, that's a good place to start looking for it."

"I was thinking," Ronnie said.

"Oh, oh," Lamont said.

Ronnie ignored him. "Sokolov would have told the Russians what's on the map."

"Maybe not," Nick said. "He could've died before they got it out of him. If they know what's on it, why try to steal it from Selena?"

"They'd want to be sure Sokolov told them the truth. That he wasn't lying to make them stop."

"If he told them what was on the map, the Russians will have the same idea I did," Stephanie said. "They'll go to Marsá Matruh to look for more information. It's a popular tourist destination. There are guided tours to the temple. At least there used to be."

"Used to be?"

"ISIS changed that. Marsá Matruh is a resort town. There are still tourists but almost no one goes out to those ruins anymore. They're close to Libya. It's not worth getting your head hacked off with a dull knife for the sake of a few pictures. ISIS is well established in Libya and they come and go as they please. You don't hear much about it because the tourism board doesn't want to scare people away."

Elizabeth picked up her pen. Nick waited for her to begin tapping it on her desktop.

"We have to take a look at those ruins," Selena said.

"People have been climbing over them for years," Ronnie said. "If anything's there, it would've been found by now."

"Not necessarily. It would be just another piece of stone with writing on it."

"I suppose it's possible," Nick said.

"You sound doubtful."

"It seems to me someone would have noticed by now if another tablet was there."

"You could be right," Elizabeth said, "but we need to check it out."

"It's a real long shot," Nick said.

"It's the only shot we've got."

"Am I in on this one?" Lamont asked.

"No. I want you healthy before you go back out in the field. There's plenty for you to do here." Elizabeth turned to the others. "Nick, you and Selena and Ronnie will go. Keep an eye out in case the Russians decide to follow up. Be careful. I don't want any of you showing up in one of those ISIS videos."

CHAPTER 16

Valentina Antipov cast a critical eye at her reflection. She brushed a speck of dust from her uniform. The four small gold stars on her shoulder boards marked her recent promotion to captain. In the mostly male world of Russian security, it was high acknowledgment.

The dark olive green color of her uniform went well with her deep green eyes. Her long, dark hair was coiled tightly at the back of her head in accordance with regulations. The jacket felt tight across her chest but that couldn't be helped. She picked up the hat, careful not to touch the gleaming visor, admiring the gold and red badge and red piping. It added a touch of color and elegance to the uniform and spoke of authority and tradition.

Today was a special occasion. She was to receive the Medal of the Fatherland, First Class, with Swords. It was an important award, about as good as it got in peacetime. President Vladimir Orlov himself would pin it on. Like the promotion, the medal was an acknowledgment of her work in the Balkans and Germany during the winter just past.

With a final quick check in the mirror, Valentina left her apartment and locked the door behind her. She went down the stairs to the street. A black Lincoln limousine waited to take her to the ceremony in the Kremlin. Modern American cars had taken the place of the aging Zils that once shepherded the elite of Russia around Moscow. A young corporal saluted and held the rear door open for her. Valentina wasn't surprised to see General Vysotsky sitting in the backseat.

"Good morning, Valentina."

"General."

Valentina's mother had been KGB, like Vysotsky. She'd died when Valentina was nine years old. Vysotsky had watched over her after that, supervising her progress and training. He'd never shown her affection that she could remember. She would not have known how to respond if he had. Valentina had long ago clamped down on her emotions, burying her desires for something more than the approval of her instructors.

Vysotsky looked her over and nodded, once.

"Good. Our president appreciates attention to detail."

"I haven't thanked you for recommending me for this decoration," she said.

"Much as I would like to take credit, it's not me you have to thank."

"Who, then?"

"President Orlov. He decided to give you this after I explained to him how your actions in Germany revealed the plot against us."

Valentina's long history with Vysotsky allowed her to address him with familiarity, at least in private. A glass window separated the driver's compartment from the rear. Even so, Valentina suspected everything said in the car would be recorded. She kept her voice neutral and her thoughts to herself.

"It is good that our president was able to call back the forces he was forced to deploy."

The truth was that Orlov had launched an unprovoked invasion of the Baltic states. He'd been tricked into thinking NATO and the West were too weak and too unwilling to respond. Anyone who made the mistake of pointing out that Orlov had been duped would soon find themselves spending time in Lefortovo prison.

Vysotsky, just as aware as Valentina that the car might be bugged, nodded agreement.

"President Orlov only wants peace with the West."

The car entered the Kremlin grounds.

"Where are we going?"

"The president has chosen the Armory for the presentation."

Valentina had expected to be taken to the Senate building, where Orlov had his office and where many official functions took place. Instead, the driver guided them toward the Kremlin Armory and stopped at the entrance. An officer wearing the rank badges of a major waited for them outside. He saluted as Vysotsky got out of the car.

"General. Captain. Please follow me. The president is waiting."

Construction of the current Armory building had started in 1844. It had always been a museum housing prized artifacts of Russian history.

They found President Orlov standing in front of the ivory throne of Ivan the Terrible, the first Czar of Russia. An aide and a photographer stood not far away. Orlov had his hands clasped behind his back, contemplating the elaborate carving on the throne.

A brilliant diplomat and a ruthless general, Ivan the Terrible had single-handedly created the Russian Empire. His nickname was well deserved. Paranoid and mentally unstable, Ivan was remembered as much for barbaric cruelty as for diplomatic successes.

Valentina had never been in the museum. She looked at the magnificent throne and then at Orlov. His expression was rapt. Nearby was a display case holding the Imperial Crown of Czarist Russia. The magnificent crown glittered with gold and priceless jewels.

He'd like to be sitting on that throne, she thought, *wearing that crown.*

Orlov turned to her and smiled. His flat, blue eyes almost twinkled. He could have been someone's favorite relative, but Valentina was not fooled. Behind the twinkle was a shrewd and calculating presence. Having Orlov turn his attention to you was like being in a room with a half domesticated wolf. You could never be quite sure what the wolf was going to do.

"Look at that, Captain." He gestured at the throne. "The man who sat there is an inspiration for us all. His vision founded our nation."

"Yes, Mister President. A man to admire."

The lie came easily. Valentina thought Ivan the Terrible was a butcher, a madman like Stalin. She didn't share the thought out loud. Everyone knew Orlov admired Stalin.

For such a powerful man, the Russian president was not impressive in size, not even as tall as Valentina. She knew he was much stronger than he looked. The Russian media liked to point out Orlov's physical prowess, his ability to swim long distances and lift heavy weights.

Briefly, she wondered what he'd be like in bed.

Probably quick to finish and quick to leave.

His mind still on Ivan, Orlov said, "More than admire. He is a man we should strive to emulate, committed to Mother Russia and her role as the greatest power in the world."

"Yes, Mister President," Valentina said again.

"It is young officers like you who are the future of our country, Captain," Orlov said. He turned to Vysotsky. "Do you not agree, General?"

"Yes, Mister President. Captain Antipov is one of our best."

"I knew your mother, Captain. We were in the KGB together."

Orlov had reached the rank of Lieutenant Colonel before resigning to enter politics.

He knew my mother. He must know everything about her. Everything about me.

It was not a comfortable thought.

Orlov gestured and the aide stepped forward, holding an open box with Valentina's medal. It was round and gold, the size of a large coin. The ribbon was a dark, earth red. In the center was a double-headed Russian eagle, overlaid on an enameled knight's cross that matched the color of the ribbon. The medal was topped with two crossed swords. Orlov lifted it from its silk cushion.

"Captain Antipov." Orlov's voice turned formal.

"Sir." Valentina stiffened to attention.

"You are awarded the Medal of the Order for Merit to the Fatherland, 1st Class with Swords, for exceptional service. Your courageous actions have strengthened our nation and contributed to public order and safety. Wear it with pride."

Orlov reached up and pinned it over her left breast. The camera flashed as the photographer took his shots. She felt Orlov's hand linger on her breast. He stepped back.

"Thank you, Mister President. I will try to live up to this honor."

"I am sure you will, Captain."

The aide said, "Mister President, it is almost time to meet with the ambassador from Burundi."

"Captain, you must excuse me. General."

Vysotsky and Valentina saluted.

When he had left the room, Vysotsky said, "I think he likes you."

Valentina remembered the feel of Orlov's hand on her breast.

I hope he doesn't like me too much.

CHAPTER 17

Nick, Selena and Ronnie flew into Cairo on diplomatic passports, posing as UNESCO officials reviewing potential world heritage sites. Their luggage wouldn't be searched by customs. They'd brought their handguns with them.

The connecting flight touched down three hours later at Marsá Matruh. They rented a Land Rover at the airport.

"We need tools," Selena said, "in case we have to dig. "

"If anything's deep we won't find it," Nick said.

"I wasn't thinking of deep. But if something is part way exposed, a shovel might come in handy."

They stopped at a store on the way to their hotel and bought a shovel.

Selena had booked a four-star hotel on the Mediterranean coast. It turned out to be a tourist trap decorated in marble and gilt. An enormous crystal chandelier loomed over the lobby. The decor was supposed to convey wealth and elegance. It didn't quite work.

"This place looks like a Vegas casino, only chintzier. Way over the top," Ronnie said.

Nick looked up at the chandelier. "At least it's not all pyramids and pharaohs."

"Would you rather be in a hostel somewhere?" Selena asked sweetly. "Maybe a tent out on the desert?"

Ronnie held up his hands in protest. "Hey, I'm not complaining."

"It is a little overdone," Selena said, "but it will be comfortable."

"Comfort is good," Nick said.

The rooms were on the fifth floor. Nick and Selena took a suite. Ronnie was in a single room down the hall.

The central sitting area of the suite featured a desk, mini bar, couch and chairs. The room looked out over a pool surrounded by tables shaded by palm thatched umbrellas. A long, thatched bar with wooden stools added to the generic resort feel. Beyond the pool was the Mediterranean. The hotel could as easily have been in the Pacific or the Caribbean as in the Middle East. Past the pool, a white sand beach crowded with sunbathers gleamed in the sun. The fear of terrorist attacks wasn't making much of an impact here.

Nick stood at the window looking out at the scene. "Lot of people out there. I don't see any Westerners, just locals."

Ronnie and Selena joined him.

"What about him?"

Selena pointed at a cadaverous man sitting at the bar wearing a tan suit and a brimmed hat.

"He looks like that movie actor, what's his name," Ronnie said. "You know, the guy that played in those black and white horror movies."

"Boris Karloff," Nick said.

"That's him."

Selena sat down on the couch.

Nick sat down next to her.

Selena said, "They get sandstorms here, don't they?"

"They get them in Cairo, they must get them here."

"Big ones?"

"I suppose so. Why?"

"It would explain why no one has noticed what we're looking for. Sand could have covered it up."

"If it's buried we'll never find it."

Ronnie looked at his watch.

"Must be time to eat."

"Not yet, amigo," Nick said. He held up a hotel brochure from the coffee table in front of the couch. "Says here the restaurant doesn't open for another two hours."

"There are snacks on top of the mini bar," Selena said.

Ronnie went over to the mini bar and picked up a tiny package of cashews. Prices were listed in Egyptian pounds.

"Sixty pounds. How much is that in dollars?"

"An Egyptian Pound is worth about twelve or thirteen cents," Selena said. "So that bag of nuts is a little less than eight dollars."

"Eight bucks for a dozen nuts." Ronnie shook his head. He picked up a small plastic bottle of water. "Water is a deal, only fifty pounds."

"Not much different from anywhere else," Nick said. "Did you ever find a mini bar where things were cheap?"

"Come to think of it, no."

Ronnie took a package of nuts from the rack. He opened the door of the refrigerator and took out a Coke.

"I'll have one of those," Nick said.

Ronnie tossed him a can. Nick popped the tab and the soda sprayed out over him.

"Damn it, Ronnie."

Selena smothered a laugh. "When do we head out to the ruins?"

"Tomorrow morning. I was thinking around eight."

"Cool. We'll have time for breakfast," Ronnie said.

That night Nick and Selena lay in bed. A gentle breeze that smelled of seaweed and saltwater came through the open windows on the balcony. A silvery moon cast soft light into the darkened room.

Selena lay with her head on Nick's shoulder, her arm stretched across his chest.

"It's almost like a vacation," she said.

"When was the last time we had a vacation?"

"That's easy. We haven't. Every time we try, something happens and we get called back."

"When this mission is over, we have to take time off. I'm getting burned out."

"Me too." After a moment she said, "Do you think what we do makes a difference in the long run?"

"The way our so-called world leaders run things? I doubt it. I'll settle for the short term."

"I'm starting to wonder if it's worth it," Selena said.

"Thinking about what we do reminds me of a song."

"Which one?"

"*The Thrill is Gone*. B.B. King."

"He was singing about a lover, not a job."

"Whatever."

Nick turned on his side to face her.

"I'll tell you one thing."

"What's that?"

He kissed her. "When I look at you, the thrill is definitely not gone."

They didn't talk much after that.

CHAPTER 18

Vysotsky summoned Valentina. Coming into his office, she saw a half empty glass of vodka on his desk. This early in the morning it meant trouble.

"Valentina. You are looking lovely, as usual. Sit."

Vysotsky gestured at a chair near his desk. She sat.

"It will interest you to know the FSB has taken an interest in your sister."

"My sister? She is in Russia?"

"No. She's in Egypt. Volkov has sent people after her."

"Why?"

"She has a map he wants. Volkov sent three of his agents to America in an attempt to get it. His operatives underestimated your sister's skills."

"She killed them?"

"She did. Now he has a problem. She will be on full alert but it's not enough to make Volkov back off. Sending agents to Egypt means he's determined to get the information from her any way he can."

Valentina affected indifference. "What has this got to do with me?"

"Oh, please, Valentina. Don't pretend you don't care, I know you too well. Your sister is important to you. You demonstrated that in Vienna and Germany."

"She is our enemy. I can't help our blood relationship. I admit, I think about her sometimes."

"That is only natural. If I thought the situation in any way compromised your loyalty, we would not be having this kind of conversation."

The unspoken threat was clear.

Vysotsky continued. "I will be truthful with you. I don't know why this map is important to Volkov but I will not let him have it. I am sending you to Egypt. Try to find out why she is there."

"What if Volkov's men do something stupid?"

"Do not intervene unless it can't be avoided. However, Volkov must not have an opportunity to question her."

"Am I authorized to use lethal force?"

"Did I say that? Use your best judgment."

He's covering his ass, in case somebody is listening. But he's not covering mine.

"Understood."

"Harker's people are staying at a hotel on the Mediterranean coast. You are leaving this afternoon. Do you want backup?"

"You know I work better on my own."

"I thought you would say that."

Vysotsky opened a drawer, took out a flat package and pushed it across the desk at her. He ticked off the contents on his fingers.

"Your tickets and hotel reservation. Location of the hotel where the Americans are staying. A car reservation at the airport. Money, Egyptian and American. Your passport."

"Who am I supposed to be?"

"You are a representative of a Moscow travel agency seeking new destinations for your clients."

"Weapons?"

"A package will be waiting for you in your hotel room."

"Will the Egyptians know I'm there?"

"No."

"Good."

"Do you have any questions?"

"Do you want me to question my sister if there's an opportunity?"

"I want you to stay away from her."

"Something could happen that makes it necessary."

Vysotsky looked at her. "Make sure it doesn't."

CHAPTER 19

At the desk of the hotel, the clerk gave them directions to the ruins and assured them it was safe to visit because the government had posted guards for the protection of tourists.

As they left the lobby Ronnie said, "I sure feel safer now."

They were doing their best to look like tourists. It wasn't hard. No one would think they were anything but what they appeared to be. Selena wore loose slacks and a lightweight, long-sleeved shirt to protect her skin from the sun. A wide brimmed straw hat and large sunglasses completed the image of a foreign woman on vacation.

Nick and Ronnie wore jeans, desert boots and loose, short-sleeved shirts. Baseball caps and sunglasses rounded out their outfits. They might have been brothers. No one would mistake them for locals.

Stalls filled with goods lined the road leading out of town. They petered out after the first kilometer. Except for the potholed highway, there was nothing to see but the Mediterranean off to the right and empty miles of sand to the left. The area was deserted. The roadside stands they saw along the way were shuttered. Faded signs proclaimed souvenirs and guide services in Arabic and tortured English.

The air conditioner in the Rover didn't work. A hot wind coming through the open windows smelled of dust and heat and provided little relief.

They passed an abandoned building advertising bottled water, food and souvenirs. Slogans in Arabic had been spray-painted across the front.

"I wonder where all the people have gone?" Selena asked

"It's because of ISIS," Nick said. He took one hand off the wheel and wiped sweat away from his forehead. "Out here, you're either with them or against them. If you're with them, you're probably off fighting in Libya. If you're against them, you're either a slave or dead."

Selena looked at a map she held in her lap. "Libya's not far away. We should reach the ruins soon."

Ronnie pointed ahead. A low building stuck up from the flat monotony of the coastal plain.

"That must be it."

They reached the temple complex ten minutes later. Nick parked in a paved lot big enough for a hundred cars. It was deserted except for a dented Volkswagen camper bus and a military jeep.

At one time this had been an important temple. The ruin was impressive. A dozen broken columns lined a wide forecourt. Three massive columns carved to represent date palms stood at the entrance, supporting an intact, flat roof. Each column was fifty feet high.

The sun beat down on the ruin, making it shimmer with golden light. The interior of the temple looked shady and inviting.

A bored attendant took a small entrance fee from them. Two soldiers sat nearby, playing a desultory board game in the shade of an awning stretched out from the side of the attendant's shack. Their rifles were propped against the wall.

"Do not wander far," one said as they walked by. "Touching anything inside is forbidden." He gave Selena a lewd look. "Perhaps you would like a private tour of the ruins?"

"I don't want one, but would you like to show my husband around?"

The guard looked confused. His companion laughed.

When they were out of earshot Nick said, "You couldn't resist, could you?"

"Did you see the way he looked at me? I wanted to slap him."

They reached the forecourt and stopped. Selena looked up at the temple and the inscriptions along the walls.

She shook her head. "This can't be the right place."

"What do you mean?" Nick asked. "This is the spot marked on the map."

"That mark is only an approximate location. Stephanie scanned the area marked on the map and found this temple. It's in about the right spot, so we all assumed this was what was meant. But this is too new, too recent. I'd guess the building dates to eleven or twelve hundred BCE, during the New Kingdom period. The pillar in the photograph goes back to King Menes, two thousand years before that. No way the Russian who marked that map found it here."

"Maybe this was built over an earlier site."

"That's possible. But if it was, they would've torn everything down and used the materials in the new building. That was common practice in ancient Egypt. Look at this place. They would never have left that column lying around."

"So what do you want to do?"

"We're here. We might as well go in but I don't think we're going to find what we're looking for."

The interior was cool and dim, a pleasant change from the heat and harsh light outside. The walls were painted with hieroglyphics.

Selena studied the writing. "I was right. This was built in the reign of Ramesses X. That puts it almost at the end of the New Kingdom."

Ronnie said, "Nothing on those walls that says 'this way to Atlantis?'"

"Smartass. It would make things a lot easier, wouldn't it? This is a dead end."

They went outside and back to their car. Another vehicle had pulled into the parking lot. A man and a woman were getting tickets. They looked European. The soldiers had quit their game and given in to boredom.

"You notice those M-16s they got?" Ronnie said.

"Dirty," Nick said.

"My DI would turn purple and scream if he saw someone with a rifle like that."

"Mine would have the poor bastard doing push-ups while he was yelling at him."

"With his foot planted in the middle of the guy's back."

"Yup."

"Are you two done remembering the good old days?" Selena studied the map. "If this is even close to accurate, that spot where the pillar was found has to be nearby."

Nick gestured at the empty desert stretching away to the horizon. Heated air rose in shivering ripples from the sands.

"We can't go wandering around out there hoping to stumble on it."

"If there's another ruin, the ticket taker might know where it is."

"Then let's go ask him."

"You wait here. He's more likely to tell me if you're not standing around looking threatening."

"Threatening?"

"I saw the way you looked at that guard when he offered to give me a private tour."

"I wouldn't call that threatening. Annoyed, maybe."

"If you say so. I'll be right back."

Katerina Rostov and Dimitri moved away from the ticket shack toward the temple. They pretended to be interested in the architecture.

Selena got out of the car.

"There she is," Katerina said.

"How do you want to handle it?"

"We can't do anything here. We watch. And wait for an opportunity."

"She's going over to the shack."

The two Russians watched Selena talking to the attendant.

"She slipped him a bribe," Dimitri said. "Now he's talking to her like they're old friends."

"She's going back to the car."

They waited until the car left the parking lot and headed west, toward Libya. Katerina and Dimitri walked back to the shack.

"Excuse me," Katerina said. "We wondered what our friends were talking to you about."

"Friends?"

"Well, not friends exactly, but we're all staying at the same hotel."

Katerina slipped a hundred pound note across the counter. It disappeared under the attendant's hand.

"They wanted to know if there were any other ruins in the area."

"Are there?"

The attendant seemed disinterested. Katerina slipped another note across.

"Yes, there is a much smaller temple a few kilometers from here, but it is not visited much. I would not advise it."

"Why not?"

The attendant shrugged. "Some people do not like foreigners around here. The place is isolated."

Perfect, Katerina thought.

"Where is this ruin?"

"You go out to the main road and turn west toward the border. Two kilometers from here there is a track turning south into the desert. Follow that for another five kilometers and you'll come to it. But there is not much to see. A few broken columns, some stones. The track is rough. I do not advise it," he said again.

"Thank you," Katerina said.

The attendant watched the woman and the man go back to their car. They pulled away from the lot and turned west, as the other crazy foreigners had.

"The blond one was pretty," one of the guards said. "All those Western women are whores. I wouldn't mind trying her out."

"You couldn't afford her. Besides, she looks like she'd kick you in the balls if you tried anything," the other guard said. "Come on, I'll give you another game."

The two men settled down to their board game. The attendant went back to the magazine he'd been reading.

Nothing ever happens here, he thought.

CHAPTER 20

Blowing sand had drifted over the disused road to the abandoned ruins. The flat desert plain of the northern Sahara stretched as far as the eye could see.

"Reminds me of Iraq," Ronnie said.

Nick steered around a depression in the track. "At least there are no IED's."

"We're almost there." Selena pointed at a rough shape sticking up out of the sand.

"Must be. There's nothing else out here."

The shape was the stub of a broken column. Nick parked and they got out of the car.

Ronnie sniffed at the air.

"Smell that?"

Nick took a deep breath and looked up at the sky. The sun had a peculiar brownish halo around it. A breeze had started, like the breath of a furnace. It brought no relief from the heat.

"Yeah. We'd better do a quick search and get out of here."

"What are you two talking about?" Selena asked. "What's the matter?"

Ronnie rubbed his nose with the back of his hand. "When I was in Iraq and it was like this, it meant we were going to get hit with a sandstorm."

"There's a sandstorm coming?"

"Feels like it."

"Then we'd better start looking."

Selena went over to the broken column. She bent down to read an inscription on the weathered stone.

"This is from the right period, when Menes was king."

The wind picked up, kicking dust into the air.

Ronnie pointed south. "Here it comes."

To the south a dark, roiling cloud rose in a towering wall toward the sky. It spread across the horizon, a tidal wave of sand coming straight toward them.

"Oh my God," Selena said.

"We'll never make it back to the highway before that hits," Nick said. "Get in the car. We'll have to ride it out."

The wind grew stronger. The sand lifted up and began to move in a rippling carpet across the ground. Tiny bits and particles flitted through the air, stinging as they hit. They ran to the car and climbed in and rolled up the windows.

"Ever been in one of these?" Ronnie asked Selena. "It's an experience."

Selena watched as the ominous cloud approached.

"Do you have a cloth to wrap around your face?"

"But we're inside the car."

"That will help but it's still gonna get hard to breathe in here. Here."

Ronnie pulled a red bandanna from his back pocket and handed it to her. She wrapped it around her nose and mouth.

"Thanks." Her voice sounded muffled through the cloth.

"You look like you're getting ready to rob a bank," Nick said.

He took off his shirt. Ronnie did the same. They used the clothing to cover the lower part of their faces and waited.

The car shuddered as the leading edge of the storm struck against it. In an instant, Selena could see nothing outside the car. A dense wall of moving sand shrieked around them. The wind pounded on the car and rocked it on its wheels. The inside of the Rover began to fill with a thin haze that stuck to her skin and coated everything with a fine layer of grit. She closed her eyes against the assault and concentrated on breathing.

She tasted the Sahara as it tried to kill her. The howling of the wind made it impossible to think. Selena felt like curling up and pulling a blanket over her head, but there was no blanket and no place to curl up in.

She wasn't sure how long it had been, but after a while the storm passed. The wind died and the air cleared. It was possible to see again through the windows, except where sand had blasted the glass into silvery translucence.

Selena took the bandanna away from her face and coughed.

She handed it back to Ronnie. "You were right."

"About what?"

"About it being an experience. Is it over?"

"Yes," Nick said. "Let's check the damage."

He grunted as he pushed the door open against piled sand. When they got out of the car, the world had changed.

The Land Rover was buried to the tops of the wheels. In places the sand had stripped away the paint, exposing bare metal. The site of the ruined temple had been scoured clean, exposing a paved court and the broken remains of fallen columns that had been hidden under the sand. After five thousand years all that was left of the main building was a low outline of weathered stone.

The three of them shook sand out of their clothes. Nick looked at the car.

"Ronnie, let's start digging out. Selena, take a look at those ruins while we're doing that."

"Wish we had another shovel," Ronnie said.

"Yeah, but we don't. You take the shovel. I'll use one of the floor mats for a scoop."

While they worked to clear sand away from the wheels, Selena began examining the ruins.

The fallen columns were covered with inscriptions. They were in bad condition, weathered by the passage of time. Even so, she could read some of what had been written.

The first column Selena looked at was inscribed with a dedication to Ma'at, the goddess of justice and truth, daughter of the sun god, Ra. Ra was the most important of the old Egyptian gods, the giver of life and light.

She moved to the next column. The writing was illegible. Past the column was a broken slab of stone lying on the ground that might have once been part of a wall.

It was inscribed with Linear D.

Finding it sent a shot of adrenaline surging through her body. She began taking pictures. Once she got back to the hotel, there'd be plenty of time to make an accurate translation. Nick came over. His shirt was dark with sweat. He wasn't in the best of moods after digging sand with a floor mat.

"I want to get out of here. Have you found anything?"

"Yes." She pointed at the fallen slab. "This is that same writing. I took pictures. I haven't had a chance to look at the rest of the ruins yet."

"Hurry up, will you?"

He stomped back to the car and popped the hood. She could hear him swearing as he did something to the engine.

Sometimes he can be a real ass, she thought.

Looking through the ruins, she found no more of the linear writing. She took pictures anyway. There could be something in the hieroglyphics. She finished and went back to the car where Nick and Ronnie waited.

"I'm done."

Nick got in the car without saying anything and started the engine. It sputtered and coughed and started.

They headed in the direction of the coast. The track they'd followed to the site was buried in sand. He drove slowly. If they got stuck, AAA wasn't coming to the rescue.

Half an hour later they reached the highway.

CHAPTER 21

Elizabeth's phone signaled. She looked at the caller ID. It was Clarence Hood.

Clarence. I hope this isn't some new emergency.

The Director of the CIA and Elizabeth had become friends. They didn't always agree, but they worked well together. Both were realists about the threats facing the country. Both were dedicated to neutralizing those threats before they became reality.

"Hello, Clarence."

"Elizabeth. Have I caught you at a bad time?"

"Not at all. I was about to leave early for a change. For once, it's a slow day."

"Slow days worry me."

"I know what you mean. When it's slow, it means the bad guys are planning something."

"I was wondering if you'd like to have dinner with me this evening?"

"I'd love to."

"How about Japanese food? There's an excellent restaurant over on MacArthur Boulevard."

"The one with the fixed menu?"

"That's the one."

"I know it. They have wonderful sushi."

"Seven o'clock?" Hood said. "I'll make reservations and meet you there. There's a back room where we can have privacy, away from the public."

Both had security issues to consider. A private room was always preferable for outings in public.

"It's a date."

"Good. I'll see you then."

Hood hung up.

A date, she thought. *Is that what it is? Come on, it's only a figure of speech.*

Her mood lifted. Before the call, the only thing she'd had to look forward to was an empty brownstone and another evening of reading reports. Dinner out was a welcome change.

A little before seven she parked and went inside the restaurant. The main room was laid out as a long, narrow rectangle. Low tables lined one wall, with square cushions on the floor for seating. A sushi bar with a dozen stools took up the other side of the room. A hanging red curtain led to the back. The decor was simple, accented with polished cherry wood and discrete lighting. Everything was obsessively clean.

A polite Japanese man escorted her back to the private room. Hood was already seated. He rose when she came in. He wore a lightweight tailored gray suit and a blue and white tie.

"You're looking nice this evening, Elizabeth."

She was wearing her usual black and white outfit, nothing Hood hadn't seen before. She took the complement for what it was.

"Thanks. This is a wonderful idea. I'm glad you called."

They sat across from each other.

A waiter appeared and Hood ordered sake for both of them. There was no need to order food. The menu was Omakase. Everything would be brought one course at a time, without any say in what would be served.

When the waiter had gone, Hood took a small electronic device from his pocket, set it on the table and turned it on. It made it impossible for anyone to listen in on their conversation.

"Just a precaution," he said.

"It's a habit," Elizabeth said. "I do the same thing in public."

Hood filled her cup and then his own. "We have a lot in common, don't we?"

Elizabeth sipped. It was good sake, cloudy, unfiltered.

"Our jobs overlap quite a bit."

Hood toyed with his cup. "I was thinking of more than our work. We enjoy similar things. Take Japanese food, for example. Not everyone appreciates sushi."

Elizabeth raised her cup, enjoying herself.

"Or sake."

"Or sake," Hood said. He lifted his cup and emptied it.

When they came out of the restaurant two hours later they were both high on the rice wine.

Hood's driver held the door open for him.

"That was fun," she said. "I really enjoyed myself."

"So did I." Hood stood next to her. "Elizabeth..."

"Yes?"

Hood reached down and touched her face. Then he leaned close and kissed her.

Elizabeth was shocked. She hadn't expected him to do that. It put her at a loss for words. Instead of speaking, she kissed him back.

Hood stepped away. "Sorry, I shouldn't have done that."

"Oh, Clarence, don't be so old-fashioned. You don't have to apologize."

"I could blame it on the sake, but that's got nothing to do with it. I find you very attractive. I thought that kind of thing was over for me. I guess I was wrong."

"That kind of thing?"

"Being attracted to someone. As I am to you."

Standing in the warm Washington evening and listening to Hood's soft, Southern accent, Elizabeth felt something shift inside. It had been a long time since someone wanted to get close. The kiss had cracked open a door she'd closed long ago.

She looked at him with a new eye. Hood wasn't a bad looking man. He was in his 60s but he'd held up pretty well. He was taller than she was, but then almost everyone was. His hair had turned full gray and was perfectly cut. He wasn't wearing any jewelry except a gold watch, not even a class ring. She liked that in a man.

"I like you too, Clarence."

"I can settle for that." He smiled at her. "Let's do this again."

"Call me."

She touched him on the arm and got into her car. Hood watched her drive away.

Down the street a man with a camera got into his car.

CHAPTER 22

Valentina called General Vysotsky from Marsá Matruh. The connection over the satellite link was faint but clear.

"Two FSB agents?" Alexei said.

"I recognized one of them. She's a real bitch. Her name is Katerina Rostov."

"I know who she is. She's one of Volkov's favorites. What's Harker's team up to?"

"I don't know. They left their hotel and Rostov followed them. They headed out on the coast highway toward Libya. It's wide open along there and there's no traffic because of the threat from ISIS. There was too much chance of being spotted if I followed, so I waited near their hotel for them. It was hours before the Americans came back. Their car looked like somebody attacked it with sandpaper. Rostov and her partner were nowhere in sight. I don't know what happened to them."

"Where did they go?"

"The only thing between here and Libya is some old ruins on the coast highway. Maybe they were going sightseeing. It's a tourist attraction, there can't be anything important about it."

"I'll be the judge of that."

Valentina wanted to tell him to go to hell. Instead she said, "What do you want me to do?"

"What you have been doing. Observe. Watch Harker's team and watch Rostov."

"I can't watch them both all the time."

"You don't have to. Rostov will be watching to see what the Americans are doing, like you. You just have to be in the right place to see them both."

Easy for you to say, Valentina thought.

"Your sister and her comrades are looking for something. Volkov wants it, whatever it is. He will have instructed Rostov to get it anyway she can. Under no circumstances must she succeed."

"Do you want me to take her out?"

"Not unless it becomes necessary."

"It would simplify things."

"No, Valentina. You heard what I said. Only if necessary. Keep me informed."

Vysotsky ended the call.

Only if necessary.

Valentina was pretty sure it would become necessary. She knew Rostov by reputation. Sooner or later the woman would make a mistake that required stepping in.

Like threatening her sister.

Thinking of Selena was complicated. Where did her loyalties lie? On the face of it, it was simple enough. Selena was a spy for the main enemy. But she was also the only family Valentina had in the world.

Valentina remembered countless lonely nights when she'd wished for a family, for someone to hold her and care for her. Her mother had been an active KGB agent and was almost never home. Valentina had been brought up by KGB and SVR instructors. The curriculum didn't include family dynamics. The ideal operative had no family except the state. Until recently, that had been Valentina's norm.

Valentina was proud of her role, her uniform. She had respect. She knew people thought her cold but she didn't care what they thought. She'd found her place in the world as an instrument of Russian state policy.

Then her world had turned upside down. She'd learned she had a sister and that her father had been an American spy.

Valentina hadn't been prepared for the emotional shock that followed from the discovery. Emotions made her uncomfortable. She'd succeeded in suppressing almost everything that felt upsetting but when she discovered Selena, the brittle walls she'd built up to contain her feelings began to crumble. She'd been shocked by the sensations that surged through her when she first saw her sister in person.

Not long after that she'd kept Selena from being horribly murdered. She hadn't been prepared for how protective she'd felt, or how angry she'd been at the same time.

It was all very confusing.

Now here she was again, keeping an eye on her sister from a distance. Like before, there was a threat to the only family she had. Rostov and her companion meant no good. If the FSB wanted something, they were skilled at getting it. Valentina was under no illusions about what would happen if Rostov managed to isolate Selena and question her. Katerina Rostov was a sadist. The interrogation would be brutal. It would be easy to make the body disappear afterward.

It wasn't going to happen, not if Valentina had anything to say about it.

CHAPTER 23

"I need a shower," Selena said.

"You and me both. You go first," Nick said.

Selena didn't argue. After she finished she dried off and put on a robe provided by the hotel. Still drying her hair, she went to her laptop and turned it on. She loaded the pictures she'd taken on her phone and chose a close-up shot of the fallen slab inscribed with Linear D. She'd begun thinking of it as the language of Atlantis.

Someone had carved the inscription more than five thousand years ago. In her imagination she pictured a man in sandals and a short, white tunic, holding a hammer and chisel as he chipped away.

Who was he, the man who put these characters here? What did he look like? Was he Egyptian? Someone from a land that's supposed to be a myth?

She brought up the notes she'd made on the tablet in the French museum. The writing in the photograph was similar, but there were characters she hadn't seen before. She copied down the new symbols, adding them to the list she'd created before. When she was sure she'd noted everything new, she looked at the result.

She now had a list of thirty-six symbols and characters, each representing a concept or thought. She'd succeeded in assigning an initial meaning to most of the characters. The problem was that a symbol that meant "water" had multiple interpretations, depending on the context.

Slowly she began to piece together a sense of what was written. She lost track of time. She started when Nick came up behind her and put his hands on her shoulders. It jolted her back to the present.

"How's it going?"

"Look at this." Selena pointed at the picture on the monitor. "What does that look like to you?"

"Like an arrow pointing away from a squiggly line, with a hat under it. And three concentric circles."

"What about that round circle with the lines coming off it?"

"I suppose it could be the sun. I've seen pictures of primitive carvings that look like that."

"That's what I think. I think this is a map."

"A map of what?"

"A map that shows where Atlantis was." She traced her finger across the screen. "The squiggly line could represent a coastline. It looks a little like the coast of North Africa."

She pointed at the concentric circles.

"That character under the circles means home. The one next to it means water, like ocean. You see how the symbol for the sun is off to the side of the symbol for home?"

"Yes," Nick said, "but I don't see what it means."

"By checking your position against the sun and this map, you'd know where you were."

Nick thought about it. "If that's the case, the sun always has to be in the same position for the map to mean anything."

"Yes. It must represent a time of day. The most logical time would be noon."

"You think these people navigated using the sun?"

"Why not? Lots of ancient cultures figured out how to sail over the ocean without getting lost."

"Where's the starting point? You need someplace to start from or the map doesn't make any sense."

"I think this symbol that looks like a hat is the temple where we found the inscription. See the arrow pointing toward the circles? If the hat represents the temple, you would follow the line of the arrow toward the circles, using the sun as your reference point. That would put you way out in the Atlantic, if I'm reading this correctly."

"You know how crazy this sounds?" Nick asked. "You're telling me you just found a map pointing to Atlantis."

"It's no more crazy than us being here in the first place," she said. "If the Russians weren't taking it seriously, we wouldn't be here."

"Was there anything on that piece of rock to tell us where the archive is?"

"No."

"Then we're back to square one."

"Not exactly. If this is a map showing where Atlantis was, we might be able to find it. The archive could be there."

"If it is, it's under a hell of a lot of water. You want to go looking for underwater ruins?"

"Those three circles could be the symbol of the capital city. It's logical that the archive would be there." Her face glowed with excitement. "Think about it, Nick. We're talking about Atlantis. We'd be the first people to see it in thousands of years. This map is the key to finding it. We have to try."

"How do you intend to get down there? I can't see Harker going to the Pentagon and asking them if she could please borrow a ship to go look for Atlantis."

"We don't need the Navy," Selena said. "I know someone who has everything we need for deep-sea exploration. I can hire him. The Pentagon doesn't need to get involved."

Every time Nick managed to forget how wealthy Selena was, something happened to remind him. The kind of expedition she was talking about would cost hundreds of thousands of dollars. Maybe more. Selena's uncle had been a billionaire. His murder had brought her to the Project and left her with a fortune. She'd given a lot of it away to charity but there was still plenty left over.

All that money hadn't turned her into someone who thought she was better than everyone else. It was one of the reasons Nick loved her.

"We'd have to clear that with Harker."

"We should go home. We're at a dead end unless there's something out there in the ocean. If the Russians come here they aren't going to find out any more than we have."

"The Russians will find that temple, like we did," Nick said. "They'll come to the same conclusion. They'll go look for Atlantis."

"Then we'd better get there before they do," Selena said.

CHAPTER 24

Katerina Rostov was angry. First they'd missed the turn into the desert. Then the storm forced them to the side of the road. Then the car wouldn't start. By the time it did, it was too late to go after the Americans. There was nothing to do but go back to the hotel.

"I hate this country," Katerina Rostov said. "I'm still trying to get sand out of my hair."

She looked out the window at the street below.

"If it wasn't for the pyramids, no one would give a shit about Egypt," Dimitri said.

"I'm tired of playing games."

"What do you want to do?"

"We have to make the woman tell us what she knows. If they found what they were looking for out there, they'll go home soon. We're running out of time."

Dimitri waited. He knew better than to interrupt her while she was thinking

"If we try to take her when she's with the others it's going to go bad. We have to get her alone. In the hotel would be best, less can go wrong."

"She's always with the others."

"She'll be less alert inside the hotel. All we need to do is get her out of the room by herself."

"How about having her called down to the lobby?" Dimitri asked. "Like for a package."

"A package would be suspicious. A message might work. Something she has to pick up at the desk."

"She'll tell them to bring it up."

"There'll be a reason why they can't. Money buys anything here. It shouldn't take much to get the clerk to do what we want."

"When do we move?"

"Now."

They were headed for the door when Katerina's phone vibrated in her pocket. She looked at the ID.

"Volkov." She made the connection. "Yes, General."

"What is your status? I am waiting for your report."

"We are about to engage with the woman. I expect to have more later today."

"You are usually more efficient, Major. Make sure that you do."

Volkov hung up.

Zhopa, Katerina thought.

"What did he want?"

"To be a pain in the ass, as usual. Let's go."

The hotel where the Americans were staying was only a few blocks away. Outside the entrance, Katerina turned to Dimitri.

"You go in before me. Meet me at the elevators in back, away from the desk."

Dimitri went in. Katerina followed him in a minute later. She went up to the desk, where a clerk waited behind the counter.

"Can you help me?" Katerina said in Arabic.

The clerk looked at her. She couldn't hide her foreignness but she'd covered her hair with a plain scarf. It seemed to show respect for Islamic custom but it was only camouflage. Katerina had no respect for Islam or any other religion.

"How may I be of assistance?" the clerk said.

"A friend of mine is staying here. I want to leave a message for her."

"There is a house phone over there." He pointed. "You can use it to call her or leave a message."

"She may be with the people she's traveling with. I don't want them to know I'm here. I want to leave her a note. Could you call up to her room and tell her there's a message waiting down here?"

Katerina had an American twenty dollar bill barely visible under her fingers. She slid it across the counter toward the clerk.

With a casual movement the clerk made the bill disappear.

"What is her name, your friend?"

"Connor. Or she may have registered under her married name as Carter. She is a blonde foreigner. I don't know her room number."

"She's in 514. I know who she is. Where is your note?"

"Do you have a piece of paper I can write on?"

The clerk reached under the counter and brought out a piece of paper and an envelope with the hotel logo.

"Compliments of the hotel."

"*Shukran.*"

Katerina wrote. She folded the paper and sealed it in the envelope. She wrote Selena's name on the outside and handed it to the clerk.

"*Shukran,*" Katerina said again. *Thank you.*

The clerk watched her walk away.

Her skirt is too short, he thought. *At least she put on a scarf. Her Arabic wasn't bad.*

He picked up the house phone and dialed Selena's room.

CHAPTER 25

Elizabeth was heading back to her desk with her first morning cup of coffee when Stephanie came into the office holding a newspaper under her arm. She looked grim.

"I think you'd better see this."

"What's the matter, Steph?"

Stephanie handed her the folded paper.

"Take a look."

Elizabeth opened the paper, a Washington tabloid that thrived on Beltway scandal. On the front page was a picture of Elizabeth and Hood locked in what looked like a passionate embrace.

CIA DIRECTOR IN LOVE TRYST

CIA director Clarence Hood was caught last night fondling an unknown female companion outside an expensive Washington restaurant. Seems that Hood has been spending his taxpayer dollars on wine, women and song. That's okay, Director. We won't tell anyone. Let's hope the lady isn't a Russian spy.

"Jesus," Harker said. "Fondling."

She sat down, her coffee forgotten. A headache began, quick and sharp.

"What were you thinking?" Stephanie said.

"What do you mean, what was I thinking? We came out of the restaurant and he kissed me."

"Don't go defensive on me, Elizabeth. We're going to have to do some damage control."

"What control? There isn't a damn thing we can do that won't make it worse for Clarence."

"What about you?"

"What about me? You saw what it said. I'm the 'unknown female companion.' It's Clarence who has the bigger problem."

"It's only a question of time until they figure out who you are," Stephanie said. "There are plenty of people who would love to see you knocked down."

"I wonder if he's seen it yet. I'd better call."

She got her phone out of her purse and dialed Hood's number. He picked up on the second ring.

"Good morning, Elizabeth."

"Have you seen the morning papers?"

"I have. I was about to call you."

"How do you think we should respond? They may not know who I am yet, but your enemies are going to come after you with their knives out. This is the kind of thing those idiots on the Hill love to get their hands on."

"There isn't much we can do. Any action we take will make things worse. We'll have to ride it out."

"And if the politicians come after you?"

"I'll deal with that as I have to. Even the Director of the CIA is allowed to have a personal life."

"All they have to do is insinuate suspicious activity and start one of their endless investigations."

"There's one thing they need to take into account," Hood said.

"What's that?"

His voice took on a dark edge Elizabeth had never heard before. It reminded her that Hood headed up one of the most powerful government agencies in the world.

"Their personal lives won't hold up to public scrutiny. By going after me, they're going after the Agency. It's not a good idea to take on the CIA. If they try to bring either one of us down over a kiss, they'll find they've opened Pandora's box. I won't let them involve you."

"I always wanted a knight in armor."

Hood chuckled. "If they come after us, they'll be the ones that need armor."

"What do you think the president will do?"

"I haven't heard from him yet, but the day is young. Rice will back us up. He doesn't like Congress any more than we do. He won't be happy about it though."

"No, I don't expect he will."

"I'm sorry you've been dragged before the public eye. From time to time these vultures follow me around, hoping for an opportunity like this."

"It goes with the territory," Elizabeth said. "It hasn't happened to me before but I'm not high profile like you."

"After this you may be."

He paused. Elizabeth heard someone talking in the background.

"I have to go," Hood said.

"Let me know what the president says. For what it's worth, Clarence, that was a pretty good kiss."

"Likewise, Elizabeth. I'll call you later."

He disconnected. Elizabeth turned to Stephanie.

"Let's get back to work. This is a distraction, but I'm not going to let it interfere. At least not much."

"Unless you have something you want me to do, I'm working on the latest ISIS encryption scheme."

"That's fine. I have to go through the morning brief for the White House. Until we hear from Nick, it's back to normal."

"Normal?"

"Whatever that is."

Stephanie looked at the row of clocks on the wall.

"He should check in soon."

CHAPTER 26

Selena answered the phone.

"Yes."

"This is the front desk. There is an envelope here for you, a message."

"A message? Who is it from?"

"I don't know. There is only an envelope, addressed to you."

"Send it up, please."

"We're busy at the moment," the clerk said. "There's no one to bring it up."

"How long will it be?"

"I am not sure, Madam. A while."

Selena looked over at Nick and rolled her eyes.

"All right. I'll come down and get it."

Selena put the receiver down.

"What was that about?"

"That was the desk. Someone left a message for me."

"How could anyone leave a message? Nobody knows you're here."

"It's probably a mistake."

"Have them send it up."

"They won't do it."

"Why not?"

"The desk clerk made a lame excuse about being busy."

"I'll go down with you."

"Don't bother. It will only take a few minutes."

Their room was in the short part of an L shaped corridor. Selena came out of the room and started for the elevators, around the corner of the L. She turned the corner and saw a man and a woman waiting for her.

She had time to think *I've seen them somewhere* when the woman jabbed a Taser into her side. Selena convulsed. The electricity ripped through her, short-circuiting her nervous system. She collapsed onto the floor, twitching.

"Quickly," Katerina said.

Dimitri was a large man, a typical Spetsnaz soldier, bulked up and strong. He picked Selena up and headed toward the fire stairs at the other end of the corridor.

Back in the room, Nick was having second thoughts about letting Selena go down to the desk alone. Something wasn't right. Who would leave her a message? No one knew they were in Egypt.

His left ear began itching.

Shit, he thought.

Nick got up and left the room, running. He turned the corner of the L in time to see a man and a woman at the far end of the hall, opening the door to the fire stairs. The man carried Selena in his arms. Her arms and legs dangled loose, her head lolled.

"Hey!" Nick yelled.

He ran toward them and drew his pistol. They turned toward his shout.

Dimitri dropped Selena, reached inside his jacket and pulled out a pistol.

Nick fired, the sound rolling down the narrow confines of the hall like thunder. He missed and fired again and missed again. Bright flame leapt from the muzzle of Dimitri's gun. The bullet ripped through Nick's jacket sleeve and burned across his arm. Katerina ducked through the open door into the stairwell and disappeared from sight. The door slammed behind her.

Nick squeezed off two more shots. A red blotch blossomed on Dimitri's white shirt. He staggered back against the wall and fired. The round passed close enough to feel it go by. Nick shot him again. Dimitri dropped his pistol and slid to the floor, leaving a wide smear of blood on the wall behind him.

Quick footsteps sounded in the hall.

"Nick."

Ronnie had heard the shots and come running. His pistol was in his hand. He looked at the carnage, at Selena lying on the floor. She was conscious, struggling to regain control of her body.

"Taser," she managed.

"Shit, man, what happened?"

Nick holstered his gun.

"This guy grabbed Selena. There was a woman with him. It was that couple we saw at the temple."

Someone opened a door to a room down the corridor. Ronnie turned, pointing his pistol.

"Get back in your room," he shouted. The door slammed shut.

"We'd better get out of here, fast," Nick said. "This place is going to be swarming with cops any minute."

"You're hit," Ronnie said. There was blood on Nick's sleeve.

"Only a scratch."

They picked Selena up and went through the door into the emergency stairwell, guns at the ready. There was no sign of Katerina.

"Can you move yet?" Nick asked.

"If you hold me up."

Nick and Ronnie held her between them and started down the stairs.

Muscle control began to come back. They still had to support her. She kept a grip on Ronnie's arm.

Nick took out his phone and punched in Harker's code.

"Nick."

"Director, we have a problem. We need out of here yesterday."

Elizabeth wasted no time asking why.

"Can you make it to the embassy?"

"We're still in Masrá Matruh and the embassy is in Cairo. We wouldn't make it. Every cop in a hundred miles will be after us."

"Are you wounded?"

"No."

"How about the airport?"

"They'll have it covered by the time we get there."

"All right. Can you get to the harbor?"

"I guess we have to."

"Go to the harbor and find a boat. Head out from land and call me. I'll see what I can do."

"Copy that." Nick disconnected.

Ronnie looked at him with a question.

"She said find a boat."

They reached the ground floor. Nick cracked open the stairway door. Two cops armed with M16s were talking with the desk clerk. As Nick watched, they ran to the elevator.

"Clear." He looked at Selena. "Can you walk now?"

"I think so. If I lean on your arm."

No one was looking in their direction.

"Let's go."

They entered the lobby and hurried to the entrance and out the glass doors. Taxis were lined up outside. They got into the first one.

"Take us to the harbor," Nick said.

"You like souvenirs?" the driver said. "My brother has a shop. Real antiques. You will like."

"Just the harbor," Nick said. He handed the driver a twenty dollar bill. "No souvenirs. Get us there fast and there's another one of these for you."

That was all it took. The taxi pulled away from the hotel, into heavy traffic. Nick thought he'd seen it all when it came to the insanity of taxi drivers but the Egyptian cabbie set a new standard.

The driver wove in and out and pulled into opposing traffic to pass, squeezing back to the sound of horns and squealing brakes at the last moment before a head-on collision. More than once Nick was certain they were doomed. They reached the harbor and pulled to a stop. Selena sat rigid in the backseat, clenching the cracked vinyl. Ronnie's reddish-brown skin had gone pale. The driver turned to Nick and beamed at him. Several of his teeth were missing. A single gold crown gleamed in the ruin of his mouth.

"Very fast, no? You are happy?"

Nick forced himself to unclench his hands. He took out another twenty and gave it to the driver.

"Very fast, yes."

The driver handed Nick a card. "My brother's shop. You must come."

They watched him drive away.

"I thought we were going to die," Ronnie said.

"He almost hit that bus head-on," Selena said. "We were doing at least sixty."

"He got us here ahead of the cops. Let's find a boat."

It was late afternoon, almost evening. The sun was moving toward the horizon in a gaudy display of orange and red and gold. A cooling breeze had begun off the Mediterranean.

"Look for a boat with some range," Nick said.

"How about that one?"

Selena pointed at a fishing boat converted for tourists. The high bow and tall cabin were still the same, but the winches and nets had been replaced with tables and chairs under a faded green canopy.

A sign on the pier advertised sunset cruises. A foreign couple stood by the sign. The man was arguing with an Egyptian wearing a dirty billed cap decorated with gold braid.

As they came close, the man threw up his hands in disgust.

"Let's go, my dear. I'm not going to pay a hundred dollars for an hour on this miserable excuse for a boat."

The Egyptian made an obscene gesture and called out in Arabic as they walked away.

"What did he say?" Nick asked Selena.

"It wasn't nice. You don't want to know."

The Egyptian captain watched them coming toward him.

"You do the talking," Nick said. "Tell him we want a private cruise. Tell him we'll pay him in American dollars. Haggle with him on the price but not for long."

The Egyptian smiled at them, hopeful.

"Sunset cruise, very beautiful evening."

Selena began talking to him in Arabic. He looked surprised that she could speak his language. He answered her. Selena shook her head and replied. The captain said something else. Selena turned to Nick.

"Three hundred dollars. He wanted more."

"Of course he did." Nick took out the money. "Give it to him."

The Egyptian's smile grew wider at the site of the money. He took it and gestured at the boat.

"I am Captain Ahmed. Please, this way."

They followed him onto the boat. A boy thirteen or fourteen years old came out of the cabin.

"My son Mohammed," the captain said. "Please, be comfortable. He will bring coffee."

Five minutes later, they left the harbor. A police car pulled up at the far end of the pier as they cleared the breakwater.

Mohammed brought a tray loaded with three glasses set in filigreed metal holders and a large brass pot with a long, narrow spout. He set the tray down and placed a glass before each of them. With casual ease he moved the pot up and down, sending the scalding coffee pouring in a perfect stream into the glasses.

"Why do they do that?" Ronnie asked.

"Do what?" Selena asked.

"Pour the coffee from way up high like that."

"It helps cool it down so you can drink it."

"I thought it was just for show," Nick said.

The sea was calm. With only a light chop, it was a perfect evening for a cruise. Under different circumstances it would have been a pleasant outing. Nick walked to the stern and took out his phone. The propeller turned and vibrated under his feet.

"Director. We're away from the harbor."

Elizabeth and Stephanie were in Elizabeth's office, looking at a moving green dot on the wall monitor that marked Nick's position.

"I have your GPS marker," she said. "I need you to get farther away from shore. As far as possible in the next hour."

"All right. What do you have in mind?"

"Someone will pick you up. I'm working on it."

"That doesn't sound very encouraging," Nick said.

"You're going to have to live with it. What happened?"

"Two people came after us. I guess it was the Russians. They tried to take Selena. They hit her with a Taser and were getting away when I stopped them."

"They're dead?"

"One of them is. The other was a woman who ducked away as soon as the shooting started. We had to get out of there in a hurry. There was no time to go back to the room. You won't believe what Selena found."

"Nothing would surprise me about this mission," Elizabeth said.

"She thinks she's found Atlantis."

The call was on speaker. He heard Stephanie gasp in the background.

"Now I'm surprised," Elizabeth said.

"I'm not sure how long I can keep this boat out here."

"You were a Marine. Find a way."

"Aye, aye, Director."

Harker disconnected. Nick went back to the others.

"What did she say?" Ronnie asked.

"She's working on it. Someone will pick us up."

Ronnie looked out at the empty ocean. "In what?"

They sat drinking coffee and watching the sunset.

Selena gripped her glass in both hands.

"How are you doing?" Nick asked her.

"I've had it. I can't do this anymore."

"What?"

"You heard what I said. I'm not going to do this anymore. I'll see this mission through but after that, I'm done. Getting tasered is the last straw. Enough is enough."

The Egyptian captain interrupted.

"We go back now."

"We want to stay out a while longer," Nick said.

"No, is dark now. We go back."

"How about another three hundred dollars for a few more hours?"

"American?"

Nick took the bills out of his wallet. Another three hundred dollars was irresistible. They disappeared into the captain's pocket.

"Two hours. No more. Then we go back."

He climbed back up into the pilothouse.

"What if we need more than two hours?" Ronnie asked.

"I'll make him an offer he can't refuse."

Two hours later the sea was still empty. The captain was giving them dark looks from the bridge.

"We're going to have to persuade him to stay out longer," Nick said.

"He's beginning to worry that something isn't right," Selena said.

"We can't go back to the harbor. The cops will be waiting. I'll call Harker again."

Nick took out his phone.

Ronnie pointed off the port bow. "I don't think you need to talk to her," he said. "Our ride is here."

The dark sail of a submarine broke the surface of the sea fifty yards away, a primal shape rising like Jonah's whale from the deep. Phosphorescent water cascaded in streams off the long, rounded hull as the deck appeared. A hatch opened high on the side of the sail.

"Lamont ought to be here. He'd love this," Ronnie said.

An officer appeared at the hatch with a bullhorn. He looked down at Nick standing by the railing of the boat. His amplified voice echoed over the water.

"Are you Carter?"

Nick cupped his hands and yelled across the gap. "Present. Am I glad to see you."

"Standby."

"Looks like we're leaving in style," Ronnie said.

"I wonder how Elizabeth pulled this off," Selena said.

Captain Ahmed and his son stood open-mouthed on the bridge, gazing at the apparition.

Nick looked at the enormous shape holding position by their tiny boat. Sailors had appeared on deck. They lowered a zodiac into the water.

"I don't know how she did it," Nick said, "but I think we're going to hear about it when we get back."

CHAPTER 27

Alexei Vysotsky listened to Valentina's report. The connection from Egypt was fair at best.

"One of Volkov's agents is dead," Valentina said.

"What happened?".

"Rostov and her companion went after the Americans inside their hotel. There was a lot of shooting. Rostov got away."

"The Americans?"

"Gone. They got out fast, without taking anything with them. I got into their room before the police. I have a laptop computer and notes my sister made. She was working on a translation."

"Do you know where they went?"

"No. They'll be as far away from here as possible. It's bad for business when people get shot in the hotel. The Egyptians are angry."

"It will be difficult for them to escape. Come home."

My sister is in trouble.

"I should stay here," Valentina said. "We have to know if the Egyptians catch them."

"There are others who can do that, Captain Antipov. You have your orders." Vysotsky hung up.

The bottle of vodka was on his desk, next to an empty glass. He poured a drink. The night outside his window was clear and hot. The overworked air-conditioning in the building strained against the humidity of a Moscow summer. Alexei's uniform jacket was draped on the back of a chair. He'd unbuttoned his collar. A fan on his desk blew warm air over him, but it didn't help much.

He considered what Valentina had told him. Volkov had overstepped himself again. Alexei thought about how he could use what had happened against the FSB director.

The Egyptians were lax in many ways, but their security service was professional and efficient. It wouldn't take long to discover that the dead body in their hotel was a Russian agent. Once they made the connection, the Egyptian government would call in Moscow's ambassador and lodge a strong protest. It was the kind of incident that threatened relations.

The Federation was negotiating with Cairo for a multibillion dollar weapons purchase. The French and Americans were offering their own wares at the same time. Even the Chinese were angling for a sale. The Egyptians had plenty of options to choose from. Volkov's indiscretion could sabotage the deal. Even if it didn't, Cairo would drive a harder bargain as a result.

President Orlov was going to be unhappy with Volkov. The thought made Alexei smile. It was never a good thing when Vladimir Orlov was unhappy with you.

Alexei sipped his vodka. The first thing was to make sure the president learned of Volkov's recklessness. It required a careful approach.

Orlov was well aware of the rivalry between the directors of the two services and encouraged it. It was important he didn't think Alexei was simply undercutting his rival. Volkov would try to make it look as though what he'd tried to do in Egypt was something Alexei should have done instead. He would say his agent had been killed in heroic service to the Motherland.

Orlov likes heroes. I can't do anything about that. But heroic deaths for no purpose are not what he wants to hear about.

Alexei needed to discredit Volkov's decision to go after the Americans. He had to plant doubt about Volkov's competence and at the same time sow a seed of suspicion.

There hadn't been enough time for Orlov to achieve complete control since the coup that had brought him to power. The military and the oligarchs could still remove him if they wished. As long as the oligarchs prospered and as long as Orlov kept the generals happy, his position was secure.

The history of Russia was an endless narrative of plots, conspiracy and murder. The times were modern, but the Russian penchant for treachery was the same as it had been when the country was ruled by Ivan the Terrible. Power in Russia went hand-in-hand with suspicion and paranoia. If Orlov suspected Volkov was plotting to set himself up as a rival for the presidential chair, it wouldn't be long before the FSB director ceased to be a problem.

Alexei took a drink. He could use what he knew about Volkov's private behaviors to go after him. Or it might be better to let Orlov's paranoia reach the conclusion Alexei wanted.

He knew how to plant the thought. It was no secret Volkov favored reestablishing the old KGB. One intelligence and security service. One director in charge of everything. Alexei understood Volkov's ambition well because he wanted the same thing, with himself as director. Supposedly the breakup of the KGB had been a move to increase efficiency. In reality, the purpose was to prevent any one man from having too much power.

Alexei would show Orlov that Volkov's adventure in Egypt was less of a patriotic effort than it was an intelligence blunder founded on ambition. He would plant the seed of suspicion that would lead to his rival's destruction.

It was a game that could have only one winner.

Alexei poured himself another drink.

CHAPTER 28

Elizabeth's day started with another blast from the tabloids about her so-called affair with Hood. She wasn't in the best of moods. The team had assembled in her office.

"What were you thinking?" Elizabeth said. "I had to call in a hell of a favor to get that sub tasked to you. You're lucky she was in the area."

"I didn't have a choice, Director. They had Selena and were about to disappear. I yelled, one of them drew on me, I shot him. What else was I supposed to do?"

Elizabeth's pen beat a tattoo on her desk.

"The Egyptians are pissed."

"What else is new?" Ronnie said. "They're always pissed, like everybody else over there."

Elizabeth gave him one of her looks. This one said *you'd better keep quiet.*

"I've used up my last chips with the Pentagon," she said. "The president wants to know why one of our submarines had to be diverted. What do you think I should tell him, Nick?"

"Tell him the truth. We were looking for a new energy source with implications for national security. The Russians didn't want us to find it and sent people to stop us. They called the shots, not us. Just don't tell him about Atlantis. That might be more information than he needs to know at this point."

The pen stopped tapping.

"Really? You don't think I should tell the president about Atlantis? That this energy source may or may not be nothing more than a legend? That we want to go looking for records that may or may not exist under thousands of feet of water? Why wouldn't I want to tell him that?"

The tips of Elizabeth's ears were turning red, a danger sign. Nick said nothing.

"Nothing more to say?"

"No."

"I didn't think so."

"It's more than a legend," Selena said.

Harker turned to her. "This better be good."

"I have pictures of the inscriptions in the Egyptian Temple. I polished up the translation during the flight home. Atlantis isn't a myth. Now that we have an idea where to look, we can pinpoint it exactly. There must still be ruins. They'll show up on a scan of the ocean floor."

Elizabeth took a deep breath, making an effort to calm herself.

"How deep?"

"It depends on where it is. The average depth of the Atlantic is about 11,000 feet but there are plenty of places where it's a lot shallower."

"How are we supposed to get to it once we know where it is? The Navy isn't going to loan me one of their research vessels. Not after sending the sub."

"We don't need the Navy," Selena said. "We can search for the stone without them. If we find what we're looking for, the Pentagon will give you a submarine and anything else you want. You'll have lots of new chips to play with."

"What do you mean?"

Selena told Elizabeth about her friend with the deep-sea exploration gear.

"I already talked with him," she said. "He's off the coast of Egypt right now, exploring the ruins of Heracleion. He's willing to work with us."

Elizabeth was getting angry again. "Do I need to remind you this mission is classified?"

"I didn't tell him what we we're looking for. Only enough to get him interested. As far as that goes, he used to be a SEAL, an intelligence officer. He has to have a high security clearance. It shouldn't be hard to read him in on a limited basis."

"I suppose you have an idea about how I'm supposed to pay for this?"

"You don't have to. I will."

Elizabeth looked at her in surprise. "Why would you do that?"

"Because I can. Because if I didn't do it, I'd regret it for the rest of my life."

"I can't permit you to do that."

"You're not giving me much of a choice."

"What do you mean?"

"If you don't give me permission, I'll resign and do it on my own."

"You can't be serious."

Selena looked at her, her expression set.

Oh, shit, Nick thought.

CHAPTER 29

Vladimir Orlov sat at his official desk in the Kremlin Senate building, reading reports. Generals Vysotsky and Volkov stood in front of the desk, waiting. Minutes dragged by as Orlov continued turning pages. Finally, he looked up at them.

"General Volkov. You are aware of the current negotiations with Egypt."

"Yes, Mister President."

Orlov's voice was calm, without emotion. It was in moments like this that you didn't want to be the object of his attention. Vysotsky's outer appearance was impassive. Inside, he was grinning.

"The sale of those arms is a matter of highest priority. Negotiations are now in serious jeopardy because of your actions. Please explain yourself."

"Yes, Mister President. The Americans are looking for something they learned about from one of our senior researchers, a traitor. I sent operatives to observe them and obtain as much information as possible. Lieutenant Arshavin died defending the Motherland. Major Rostov escaped."

"So you say in your report. It would have been easier if the traitor had not died under your interrogation. Did you discover whether or not the Americans found what they are searching for?"

Volkov looked uncomfortable. "Not yet. But..."

Orlov held up his hand. Volkov stopped talking.

"Four agents dead in the last week and you still do not know what the Americans are doing. It seems General Vysotsky has had better luck than you."

Volkov glanced at Alexei with a look of pure hatred.

Orlov continued. "I have his report here. He states that the Americans are searching for records of an ancient power source that could provide us with a strategic advantage. His operative recovered materials in Egypt that explain where it might be found. The Americans know where to look."

Volkov turned to Vysotsky. "You had someone in Egypt?"

Alexei kept his voice mild. "Your department has no mandate to pursue foreign agents outside our borders. That is the function of SVR, as you well know. When I learned what you had done, it seemed prudent to send someone. Her orders were to observe and remain undetected. Had I known your agents were going to create an international incident, I would have ordered her to intervene."

"You are a pompous ass," Volkov said.

"At least I am not an idiot. I know better than to provoke a conflict with the Americans."

"That is because one of your agents is the sister of an American spy."

"No. It is because I am not a thug like you, always ready to bring out the jackboot at any opportunity."

Before Volkov could respond, Orlov interrupted.

"Enough. I have had enough of this childish arguing. You are two of my most important officers. If you cannot find a way to cooperate, I will replace you with others who will. Am I clear?"

Both men answered at once. "Yes, Mister President."

"General Volkov. Do not let a mistake like this happen again. Have I made myself clear?"

"Yes, Mister President."

"General Vysotsky. I want to know what the Americans are doing. You are not to confront them directly unless they initiate a conflict. This is now your priority. Understood?"

"Yes, Mister President."

"Dismissed."

The two generals saluted and clicked their heels together. They left the room without looking at each other.

Orlov watched them go, thinking about Vysotsky's report and Volkov's ambition.

CHAPTER 30

Nick and Selena were downstairs at Project Headquarters, getting ready to try out the new guns.

"Why did you have to say that?" Nick said. "You put Harker in an impossible position."

"What's impossible about it?"

"Come on, you know what I mean. You gave her an ultimatum. Either she gives in and lets you do it the way you want or she has to let you resign. She's concerned about security. You should've run it by her first before you talked to this guy with the boat."

"He's not just a guy with a boat. Jeffrey is an old friend."

"He's an old friend? Is that supposed to make it all right?"

"It means that I trust him. I didn't tell him what we're looking for, only that I thought I knew where there could be a sunken city like Heracleion that hadn't been discovered."

"Did you tell him who you work for?"

"Of course not. I told him I came across a mention of the city while I was translating a hieroglyphic inscription. It's close enough to the truth that I didn't have to make up a complicated explanation."

Nick shook his head. "You should have talked to Harker first."

"You said that."

"What are you going to do if she says no?"

Selena shrugged. "What I said. I'll resign. I'm not going to pass up what may be the most exciting and important find of the century because some admiral doesn't want to give us what we need."

"You can't resign. This whole thing is classified to the hilt. Even if you did, you couldn't go anywhere near that underwater site without breaking a dozen laws."

"Then we'd better hope I don't have to," Selena said, "because I would go anyway."

They were interrupted by Lamont. He came into the room carrying two of the Heckler and Koch MP7s.

"Hey, boys and girls. You ready to try out the new toys?"

He took one look at the two of them standing there, face-to-face.

"Am I interrupting?"

"We were talking about what Selena said to Harker."

Lamont looked at Selena. "Harker's got a lot on her plate right now. She doesn't need your attitude."

"My attitude? Is that what you think this is?"

"What the hell else would it be? She's right to be pissed off at you. You talked to a civilian before you cleared it with her."

"He's no more a civilian than you are," Selena said. "He was a SEAL, like you."

"He doesn't work here. That's the difference."

"Elizabeth should be grateful. I just offered her the means to accomplish the mission."

"For someone as smart as you are, you can be pretty damn stupid sometimes."

Lamont put the weapons down on a table and left the room.

"Nice going," Nick said. "Maybe you can piss off Ronnie and Stephanie too before the day's over. I'm going after him."

Selena watched Nick leave.

What is it with everybody? I was only trying to help.

She thought about picking up one of the MP7s and shredding a silhouette downrange. But the weapon was unfamiliar to her, different from the MP5 she was used to.

Better to wait. Lamont will show me later, after he cools down. She looked again at the weapon, compact and deadly, a premium creation of German weapons engineering.

If you quit, you won't have to bother with learning new weapons. You can always go back to the lecture circuit. That will be exciting. The thought came unbidden.

Sometimes when the inner voice kicked in she wished it would shut up.

If you didn't work here, you wouldn't even know about Atlantis.

"All right," Selena said out loud. "I get it."

"Get what?" Ronnie came into the room and looked around. "Who are you talking to?"

"Nothing. I was thinking out loud."

"Where's Lamont? I thought we were going to work with the guns."

"He went off with Nick. I'll go find them."

"You really going to quit?"

"It depends on Elizabeth," Selena said.

"You should talk to her. You jumped on her pretty quick." Selena sighed. "Et tu, Brutus?"

"You know I'm right," Ronnie said. "She's going through a hard place right now."

"What about?"

"Haven't you read the papers?"

"Not since we got back."

"The tabloids are after her. Well, after the CIA. They got a picture of her and Hood smooching outside a restaurant."

"Elizabeth and Hood? Really?"

"Yup."

"Oh. That's not good."

"Yup."

"I guess I'd better go talk to her," Selena said.

"That would be a good idea."

Selena went upstairs and knocked on Elizabeth's open door. Harker was writing. She looked up.

"What is it, Selena?" Her voice was unfriendly.

"Have you got a minute?"

Elizabeth gestured at a chair near her desk.

"I want to apologize," Selena said. "I should have talked to you before I talked to my friend."

"Yes, you should have. Is that all?"

She's not making it easy.

"I also want to say that I'm sorry I said what I said. About resigning. Whatever you decide about using him, I can respect that."

Elizabeth put her pen down. "You're withdrawing your threat to quit if I don't go along with it?"

"Yes."

"You gave me an ultimatum. I can't have that kind of insubordination on the team."

"I know. It won't happen again."

"Damn it, Selena, what's going on with you? Are you and Nick having trouble? Because if you are, I need to know it. You've been preoccupied since you got back from Germany."

Selena knew she was right. Thoughts of resigning had been popping up more and more. She hadn't talked much about it with Nick. The few times she'd brought up the possibility he'd reacted badly.

"I've had plenty of time to think about what happened over there. I was helpless and they were going to cut me up a piece at a time and make a movie out of it. Sometimes I wake up at night with that movie playing through my head."

"You need to see somebody. I don't have to tell you about PTSD."

"I've been putting it off."

"Don't put it off any longer. That's an order."

It felt like a defeat. "All right."

"What's the name of your friend with the boat?"

"Jeffrey Sexton. He owns a vessel that used to belong to the NOAA. Right now he's off the coast of Egypt researching Heracleion. He's well-equipped. State-of-the-art computer surveying equipment, a deep sea ROV and pretty much everything we'd need."

"What did you tell him?"

"Only that I'd come across a reference to a sunken city that was at least as old as Heracleion. I said I wanted to find it and that I would pay all the expenses. He knows I've done some serious diving. I didn't say anything about Atlantis or what we're looking for."

"If I decide to bring him on it won't be necessary for you to pay him. We have funds that can be used."

You should have thought of that, Selena's inner voice said.

Elizabeth continued. "I'll check out his background. If he clears, we'll set up the mission. Is there anything else?"

"No. Only that I really am sorry."

"Apology accepted. Make that appointment to see someone."

It could have been worse, the voice said.

CHAPTER 31

Stephanie ran a satellite scan of the ocean floor, using Selena's ideas about where to look. Near the Azores, she found regular shapes on the seabed that might be ruins. Whether or not they were the remains of Atlantis remained to be seen, but they were in the right place.

Everyone met in the ops center beneath Elizabeth's office to plan the mission.

"Selena's friend is a civilian," Elizabeth said. "His clearance checks out and he was a SEAL, so that makes it easier. However, I don't want him to know what we're really doing. If he does find out, we'll deal with it then. Do your best to conceal your real objective."

"Jeff won't be easy to fool," Selena said. "He's experienced and intelligent. When we find those ruins he's going to start asking a lot of questions. It won't take him long to put it together. I think you should count on him discovering it's Atlantis."

"I can live with that. The secrecy agreement will forbid him from releasing information about what you discover without permission. But I don't want him to know there's more to it."

"That shouldn't be too difficult."

"You said that he has an ROV on board?" Elizabeth asked.

"Yes. The first thing to do is send it down and get some pictures. Scout the area. We can plan the dive after that."

"I don't want his people diving on the ruins. Selena, you're the only one I want going down there. If..." She stopped. "What?"

"I won't dive alone. It's suicide if it's deep. Someone has to be with me."

"That's easy," Lamont said. "I'll go with you."

"You can't go," Nick said. "Your lungs are shot up."

"Still breathing, aren't I? As long as I have good gear and use a little caution, it won't be a problem."

"When did you ever use caution?"

"Whenever you didn't. Means I've had plenty of practice."

Ronnie laughed out loud.

Elizabeth was concerned. "Lamont, are you sure you can handle this? It hasn't been that long since you were in the hospital."

"I'm fine, Director. It's the only practical solution if you don't want some civilian going down there with her."

"If there has to be someone with me, I'd rather it was Lamont," Selena said. "I can trust him. We've been down together before."

"I'll think about it," Elizabeth said.

"What's our primary objective?" Nick asked.

"To find the archive Sokolov mentioned in his letter. Even better, find the stone they used to put this mysterious energy to work."

"We're talking about a ruined city that disappeared thousands of years ago. It's going to be covered with silt. The chances of finding either one are about zero."

"We still have to look."

"What about the Russians?" Selena said.

"What about them?"

"My computer was in our room. Everything was on it. If they found it, they know as much as we do."

"There isn't anything we can do about it if they did. It means you have to stay alert out there. Treat it as a high risk mission."

"If they have Selena's computer, they'll show up on site," Nick said.

"It's possible."

"What are the rules of engagement if they do?"

"Stay out of their way if you can."

"And if we can't?"

"Do what you have to do," Elizabeth said, "but don't get caught doing it."

CHAPTER 32

The R/V *Sexton's Dream* gleamed white in the Egyptian sun, two hundred and thirty-five feet of ocean high tech. The bridge bristled with a complex array of antennas and radar. A tall mast flying an American flag on the aft deck added a Christmas tree of electronics.

A thick rectangular frame painted yellow jutted out over the water at the stern. The deck was crowded with equipment.

Several hundred yards away was another research vessel that dwarfed *Sexton's Dream*. The bridge sat on top of a superstructure that looked like a transplanted apartment house.

The launch carrying Nick and the others pulled up to a gangway that had been lowered on the starboard side. A muscular man about Nick's age and size waited for them on deck. He had brown, curly hair, a deep tan and a broad smile. He wore khaki pants, boat shoes and a red shirt open at the collar.

"Hi, Jeff," Selena called.

She waved at him, looking happy. Jeff waved back. Nick felt something ancient and hostile stir inside.

When they reached the top of the gangway steps, Selena hugged her friend.

"It's been too long," she said. "Jeffrey, this is my husband, Nick."

"A pleasure to meet you." His eyes were neutral as he studied Nick. His handshake was firm. He turned to Selena.

"I didn't know you were married."

"Late last year. We didn't send out invitations."

She introduced Lamont and Ronnie.

"Let me show you around. We're a little cramped but quite comfortable."

"How large a crew do you carry?" Lamont asked.

"Eighteen crew and three officers. Plus the scientists. We can bring as many as thirteen with us. Right now there are only five, all marine archaeologists."

"You've been studying Heracleion?" Selena said.

"Yes. We've pulled up all sorts of interesting things. Gold coins, pottery, statues. It sank around eighteen hundred years ago."

"Why did it sink?" Nick asked.

"It was built on silt accumulated from the Nile Delta. The current theory is that earth tremors liquefied the base. One day it was there. Then it wasn't. There are several tectonic plates that come together in this part of the world. The whole area is seismically active. There was a 6.0 quake not long ago, right in the middle of the Mediterranean basin. We got another alert this morning. Everything from here all the way out to the middle of the Atlantic is potential quake country."

"How far down is Heracleion?" Lamont asked.

"Oh, not very far. It's an easy dive, maybe ten meters. The water is murky. No one ever noticed it until the French stumbled on it sixteen years ago."

"What's that other research ship out there?" Selena pointed off the port bow at the larger ship.

"That's the R/V *Tolstoy* out of Sevastopol."

"Russian?"

"They're with the Shirshov Institute in Moscow. Pretty glum bunch. They keep to themselves."

Jeffrey gave them the tour. The interior of *Sexton's Dream* was fitted out with a bosun's shop, a communications room, an elaborate electronic shop that looked as if it belonged at NASA, a machine shop and a lab where recovered artifacts soaked in tanks of saltwater. The bridge was crammed with computers and electronic displays.

"I upgraded everything when I bought the ship," Sexton said. "It's the best gear available, as good as what the military has. Our scanners produce accurate images of the ocean floor, even the deepest parts."

He led them down a corridor with small cabins on the side. Each cabin slept two or four. Jeffrey assigned two of them.

"Selena, you and Nick take this one. Lamont and Ronnie, you're next door."

"When's chow call?" Lamont asked.

"Two bells into the dog watch."

Lamont smiled. Selena looked confused.

"1700," Jeffrey said. "Now if you'll excuse me, I need to go topside."

"It's good to see you again."

"You too." He took Selena's hand. "Come on up when you're ready."

The cabin was hot and stuffy. Nick opened the port hole to a fresh, Mediterranean breeze that brought the rich smell of the harbor

"So that's Jeffrey," Nick said. "A ship like this, he must have quite a bit of money."

"He comes from a wealthy family. His grandfather made a fortune in timber."

"How well did you know him?"

"I told you, we went to school together."

"The way he looked at you was more than just friendship."

"Oh, Nick, it was a long time ago."

"Did you sleep with him?"

"Once."

"Because you were friends."

Selena was getting annoyed. "Yes. Because we were friends. There wasn't anything more to it than that."

"If you say so."

"There's no reason to be jealous. It's not like you."

Nick took a deep breath. "Sometimes I look at you and I think I can't be this lucky. You can't blame me for getting jealous once in a while."

Selena put her arms around him. "That might be the nicest thing anyone ever said to me."

She kissed him.

After a moment, they broke apart. "Let's go topside before this turns into more than a kiss," Nick said. "We need to tell Sexton where we want to go."

Selena took a folder with copies of Stephanie's satellite scans out of her backpack. Nick tapped on the open door of Ronnie and Lamont's cabin.

"Time to let the Captain in on what's happening."

They found Sexton on the bridge, talking with his first mate.

"We need to brief you," Nick said.

"Let's go into the wardroom."

They followed him to the room used by the ship's complement of officers. The wardroom was paneled with varnished wood and fitted out with polished brass lamps. It had the feel of another time, when ships traveled under sail and the lamps were lit with oil instead of electricity. Much of the small room was taken up by a narrow, rectangular table. They sat down at the table.

"You mind telling me what this is all about?" Sexton asked. "You've been checking on my security clearance."

Nick saw no reason to deny it. "How did you know that?"

"I have my sources. You're not out here because you're looking for an interesting dive." He looked at Selena. "Are you?"

"Why do you think that?" she said.

"Oh, I don't know. It could be that pistol you've got tucked away in the small of your back. Since when did you start packing? Although I remember you saying you wanted to shoot that philosophy professor."

"For being boring. I'd forgotten that."

Jeffrey turned to Lamont. "I guess you don't remember me. The Gulf? Operation Broken Wing?"

Lamont gave him a careful look. "Yeah, I remember you now. You were dressed like an Arab. You were the Intel officer."

"Yes."

"That was a good mission. We got our pilot back and kicked ass."

"It was a good team." Sexton paused. "It doesn't take a genius to figure out you four are a team. Except for Selena, it's obvious you three are military. Why are you here?"

"It's classified," Nick said, "and we're former military, not active. Before we go any further you need to look at this and sign it."

He pushed a piece of paper across the table. Sexton picked it up.

"A secrecy agreement? I haven't seen one of these for a while."

Sexton took a pen from his shirt pocket and signed the paper.

"You don't want to read it?"

He handed it back. "I've seen them before. Okay, what's this all about?"

"Selena, you brief him."

"How much can I tell him?"

"You can tell him what you think you found. He doesn't need to know more than that at this point."

Sexton watched the exchange. "Now I'm really curious. When we talked on the phone you said you'd found an undiscovered sunken city."

"That's right," Selena said. "What I didn't tell you is that I think I found Atlantis."

Sexton started to laugh, then stopped. "You can't be serious." He looked at their faces. "You are. I don't believe this."

"I'm almost certain the city I found was the capital of Atlantis. The only way to know for sure is to dive on it. That's why we need you."

"My sources said I was being looked at by a spook agency. They didn't know who it was but they didn't think it was Langley. Who are you working for?"

"We work for the president," Selena said. "I can't tell you more than that."

She put the folder with the scans and GPS coordinates on the table.

"Everything you need to know to find the site is here. The plan is to locate it, dive on the ruins and decide if it is Atlantis. You can't tell anybody about it. In the future, if it turns out to be Atlantis, you'll be able to claim some of the credit for the discovery. It will make your reputation. Until then, everything is black. Are you good with this?"

"What are you looking for? Wait, I know, you can't tell me because it's classified."

"That's right. You must understand that, with your intelligence background."

"Sure I do. Okay, let me see what you've got."

Selena passed the folder over to him.

"The site is near the Azores," Selena said.

They waited while Sexton took out the scans and charts and began looking through them. After a few minutes he looked up.

"No question there are ruins down there," he said. He was excited. "Atlantis. I can't believe it. We'll leave tomorrow. If these coordinates are accurate I can have us on site a week from now."

"You can't get us there sooner?" Nick asked.

"I have to take care of a few things here before I leave," Sexton said. "If I suddenly take off it will seem odd."

"I guess we'll have to settle for that," Nick said.

Someone knocked on the door. Sexton rose and opened it.

"Skipper, the harbormaster is here. He mentioned a new tax."

"Tell him I'll be right out."

"They tax you for being here?" Selena asked.

"He's looking for a bribe. Are we done for now?"

"Yes."

Sexton got up and they followed him on deck.

A small motor launch bobbed in the water alongside *Sexton's Dream*. A pudgy man with a large mustache stood in the bow. Behind him were two uniformed police officers. A sailor manned the cockpit.

"Peace be upon you, Captain," called the official in English.

"And upon you," Sexton said.

"A beautiful day, is it not?"

Nick saw one of the policeman staring at Selena. He said something to the other cop. Both of them looked at her and then at Nick.

"I understand a new permit is required," Sexton said.

"Alas, it is always so."

Sexton took a fat envelope from his pocket. "I was fortunate enough to obtain the necessary forms when I was in town yesterday. I've filled them out. They're in this envelope with the fee."

The man smiled. "Excellent, Captain, excellent."

One of the policeman came over to him and began talking. He pointed at Nick and Selena. Nick couldn't hear what he said. The harbormaster frowned and said something back. The cop looked unhappy.

The harbormaster said, "This officer will come up and retrieve it from you."

"No need," Sexton said. He handed the envelope to his first mate, standing nearby. "Take this down to him, John."

The mate went down the steps with practiced ease, handed the envelope over and returned.

The harbormaster glanced inside. The envelope vanished into his pocket. "Everything appears to be in order, Captain. I will see you again, soon."

"I look forward to it."

The harbormaster sat down and the launch pulled away. They watched it leave.

"I think that cop recognized us," Selena said.

"I think you're right." Nick turned to Sexton. "We need to leave now."

"Something you're not telling me?"

"We had a little trouble in Cairo a few days ago," Selena said.

"And now the cops are after you."

"Yes."

"Tell me," Sexton said. "This mission of yours. Does it impact national security?"

"You could say that," Nick said.

Sexton walked over to his mate. "Fire her up, John. We're leaving."

CHAPTER 33

Alexei Vysotsky's daily intelligence brief contained an article from a Washington newspaper with a photograph of Elizabeth and Hood embracing. The picture caught him by surprise.

How can she be interested in him? He's a lot older than she is...

He read the article, smiling at the implication Elizabeth might be a Russian spy. Alexei had met Elizabeth and liked her. She'd had earned his trust, up to a point. Mutual threats had forced a temporary alliance between them on two occasions. It was an unusual relationship between unlikely opponents. He was sorry she was caught up in a scandal, but she was the opposition. Anything that distracted her was good.

Alexei turned to the next item, a report from Cairo. He sat up straight in his chair.

Harker's people seen on a private research vessel. Now the boat's gone and so are they. They must be following up on the translations...

An hour later Vysotsky stood in front of Orlov's desk. The Federation president wore his usual dark blue suit, accented with a blue and white tie. The color of the tie matched his ice blue eyes. A small Federation flag on his lapel caught the light from an overhead chandelier.

Vysotsky briefed Orlov on events in Egypt.

"What do you propose, General?"

"The Americans are going to the undersea site. We should explore it for ourselves. They can't stop us and we need to know what's there. We have a suitable vessel in Egypt, the R/V *Tolstoy*. She's civilian, but she'll do what we say."

"Sit down, General." Orlov waved his hand at a nearby chair. Alexei sat.

"I have been skeptical all this talk of Atlantis would lead to much. It's obvious the Americans think it's important. You were right to bring this to me."

Alexei waited.

"Tell me," Orlov said, "how are you getting along with General Volkov these days?"

The question caught Alexei off guard.

"We have little to say to one another, Mister President. About this matter or any other. Routine exchanges of important information continue between our organizations."

"But not between the two of you directly."

"No."

"Volkov is ambitious. Would you agree?"

It was a question with consequences. Whatever Alexei said could be wrong. Orlov had always been good at spotting deception. Alexei decided on the truth.

"Yes, Mister President, I would agree. He wants to bring back the KGB, with himself as director."

"As do you, General."

Alexei's heart thumped in his chest. "I do not deny it. I think it would be more efficient if our services were under one roof again. The difference between General Volkov and myself is that I serve the Motherland with my ambition. He serves only himself."

Orlov nodded. "Had you denied it, you would now be on your way to Lefortovo."

He rose and walked over to one of the tall windows looking out over the Kremlin Gardens. He stood with his back to Alexei and his hands clasped behind his back.

Alexei rose from his chair. *Where is this going? What does he want?*

"General Volkov's ambition may be as you say. But I require proof." He turned back to face Alexei. "This adventure in Egypt may provide an opportunity."

Alexei had trouble believing what he was hearing. Orlov was giving him permission to take down Volkov, if he could.

"What do you require, Mister President?"

"I want you to form a joint operation. Assign someone from SVR to go to Egypt and report on what happens. I will instruct Volkov to do the same. Your agent should observe what Volkov's operative does. I think Volkov will make a mistake."

"Who is in command?" Alexei asked.

"You are, through your operative. I will make that clear to Volkov. Assign someone with rank."

"I would like to send Captain Antipov. She is familiar with the situation. It's because of her that we know what the Americans are doing."

"An excellent choice. Promote her to Major. That should give her enough authority."

Orlov smiled. There was something predatory about it.

Valentina, Alexei thought, *you are moving into dangerous territory.*

CHAPTER 34

Vysotsky returned to SVR Headquarters. Within an hour, Orlov's aide phoned him to tell him Volkov had assigned an agent to the operation. Alexei summoned Valentina to his office. He turned on the unofficial device that shielded the room from eavesdroppers.

"Major Antipov. I am sending you back to Egypt."

Surprise registered on Valentina's face.

"Major?"

"You have been promoted. Congratulations."

"What's the catch?"

"Valentina, you hurt my feelings. You deserve this promotion. President Orlov himself told me to give it to you."

"You and I have known each other too long for foolish games. As I said, what's the catch?"

"You will be working with one of General Volkov's operatives. This is a joint mission with FSB."

"FSB agents are a pain in the ass. They are all idiots. Who is he?"

"It's not a he. Volkov has assigned Major Rostov."

"Her? Work with that bitch? I will not do it."

Alexei sighed. "Sometimes you can be truly ridiculous. You have no choice in the matter. It's an order."

"No one works *with* Rostov," Valentina said. "She thinks the sun shines out of her ass."

"Please, Valentina, there's no need to be crude. You are in charge. Besides, your real mission isn't to work with her. It's to report on her actions."

"You want me to spy on her? I admit, that appeals to me."

"I thought it might. This is a tricky assignment for you. Orlov is watching closely. He is looking for something to use against Volkov."

"All he has to do is make it up," Valentina said.

"You are lucky no one can hear what is said in this office."

"You know it's true."

"That may be, but in this case proof is required. A conversation overheard. Perhaps an intercepted message. Proof that Volkov is disloyal and seeks his own advancement over the needs of the Motherland. Even better, something that criticizes the president in no uncertain terms."

"Whatever else Rostov is, she's experienced and careful," Valentina said. "It will be difficult to catch her out in anything as obvious as what you suggest."

"That is why I've assigned you to this operation. Because of its difficulty. Harker's team has returned to Egypt."

My sister.

"They are on their way to an underwater site to search for the remains of Atlantis."

Valentina looked at him.

"You're joking."

"I am not. The R/V *Tolstoy* is waiting for you near Cairo. She will take you and Major Rostov to the site."

"Why would they look for Atlantis?"

"They're looking for an artifact."

"What kind of artifact?"

"One that can be of use to us. That is all you need to know."

Valentina knew better than to push further.

"What are your instructions?"

"Observe the Americans. You are not to interfere unless the situation deteriorates and you have no other choice."

"Understood."

"You and Rostov leave tonight. Military transport has been arranged for you. You have proved efficient in the past, Valentina. I expect no less from you now. Orlov wants a result and he's taking a personal interest in you."

"When he pinned that medal on me, he fondled my breast. I don't like him."

"He has marked you for his inner circle," Alexei said. "It's a pool full of sharks. Find what he needs in Egypt. What protects you is your success."

"And if Rostov creates trouble?"

Alexei steepled the ends of his fingers together.

"There are also sharks in the Mediterranean," he said.

Valentina suppressed a smile.

A few miles away in FSB Headquarters, General Volkov was briefing Katerina Rostov.

"You are leaving for Egypt at 2100 hours," he said. "Orlov is playing games. He's placed an SVR operative in charge of this mission. You will be under her orders."

"Who is it?"

"Valentina Antipov. The one who got the medal after Orlov called off the Baltic invasion."

"I know who she is. She's an annoying woman and she's only a captain. How can she be in charge?"

"Orlov has promoted her to Major."

"I don't like her."

"I'm sure the feeling is mutual. However, that is the situation. You do not have a choice."

"What is it you want me to do?"

"You will stop the Americans from recovering any useful information."

"They will be working underwater. I'm no diver."

"You'll have a Spetsnaz team with you. Their job is to take care of whatever is in the water. Yours is to keep the Americans from succeeding."

"It will require a violent solution," Katerina said. "Are you prepared for whatever fallout comes from that?"

"If you do your job properly, there will not be any fallout. Unfortunate accidents happen at sea all the time."

CHAPTER 35

The *Sexton's Dream* passed through the Straits of Gibraltar. The smooth surface of the Mediterranean gave way to the endless rolling motion of the Atlantic. Selena and Nick stood at the bow. To starboard lay the massive landmark of the rock of Gibraltar. On the port side, Jebel Musa rose in the hazy distance. Ahead lay the vast expanse of the ocean, sparkling with sunlight.

"This is what Plato wrote about in his dialog," Selena said.

"What is?"

She pointed at the rock of Gibraltar and the mountain to the left. "We're passing through the Pillars of Hercules. Gibraltar is one pillar. That mountain over there in Morocco is the other. When Plato wrote about Atlantis he said it was beyond the Pillars of Hercules. It looks like he was right."

"I've never been to the Azores," Nick said.

"It's a beautiful place to visit." Selena brushed away a strand of hair. "There are nine islands, all part of the mid-Atlantic Mountain Range."

"There's a mountain range in the Atlantic?"

"It was formed by tectonic plates moving apart. The Azores are volcanic peaks of the ridge."

"That might explain what happened to Atlantis," Nick said. "What if something they did triggered a volcanic eruption?"

"A volcanic eruption? It would have to be awfully big."

"It's happened before. Like the Minoan civilization."

"Yes, but that's different. There are still plenty of Minoan artifacts to study. Ruins, everyday items, the language. Lots of things."

"Okay, an undersea earthquake then. Big enough to sink the whole civilization. We don't know how big Atlantis was. Maybe it was just an island. Don't the legends mention an island?"

"They do."

"It could've been like the eruption of Krakatoa back in the 1800s. That wiped out a large island and killed thousands of people. Or there could have been an undersea quake. Sexton said the whole area is seismically active. Unstable."

"If we find ruins, there might be something that tells us what happened," Selena said.

Two days later they reached the area pinpointed on the scans. The team crowded onto the bridge. One of Sexton's crew sat at an electronic console watching a large monitor. As the ship moved through the water, changing images in brown and yellow passed across the screen. A scale on the side of the monitor displayed ocean depth in meters. Sexton stood behind him.

"What's your plan?" Nick asked.

Sexton pointed. "You're looking at images from the side-scan sonar system. I've laid out a grid to search, based on the satellite intel you gave me. We'll work our way back and forth across the grid."

He gestured at the screen.

"You can see the variations on the ocean floor. It looks fairly smooth here. If those ruins are down there, we'll find them. There's not much to confuse the image."

"How does it work?" Ronnie asked.

"The scanner trails behind the ship," Sexton said. "The sonar sends down pulses in a fan shape. They bounce back as an acoustic reflection, recorded in slices. The computers piece the slices together and get an image."

An object shaped like a boat's hull appeared, slice by slice, five hundred meters down. It passed out of sight as the ship continued on.

"Probably a fishing boat," Sexton said. "There are a lot of wrecks out here. People have been sailing these waters for a long time."

"How long will it take us to search the grid?" Selena asked.

"The whole thing? A few days, maybe longer. But I don't think we'll have to do that. We're at the edge of the area you identified on those scans, so it might not take long."

"I'm going to check over the diving gear," Lamont said.

"I'll go with you," Selena said.

"I'll help you unpack." Ronnie followed them out as they left the bridge.

Nick stood next to Sexton, looking out through the bridge windows. There was nothing to see except the constant motion of the water. A few white clouds drifted overhead in a clear blue sky.

"How did you hook up with Selena?" Sexton asked Nick.

"It's a long story. Her uncle was murdered. We were asked to look into it."

"We've been friends a long time."

"Selena told me about it."

An image of Selena in bed with Sexton flashed unbidden in Nick's mind. It made him angry. Even though it had been long before Selena came into his life.

"She's special," Sexton said. "You're a lucky man. Me, I've never been able to settle on one woman."

Asshole, Nick thought.

The sonar operator called out.

"I've got images, Skipper."

The two men walked over and looked at the monitor. It showed a long shape on the ocean floor at a depth of eight hundred meters. As the ship moved over the surface regular shapes appeared, far below.

"That's got to be it," Nick said.

"Do you want me to keep searching the grid?"

"No, we'll start here. Get us stopped over what's down there."

As Sexton gave orders to his crew, Nick stepped outside to where the others had laid out the diving gear on the deck. The steady vibration of the engines changed as the boat slowed and stopped.

"Why are we stopping?" Selena asked.

"Sonar shows the ruins of a city below us. Or at least what looks like ruins."

"How far down?" Lamont asked.

"Eight hundred meters, give or take a few."

"We can't dive that," Lamont said. "The deepest anyone has ever gone using gas mixtures is a little over five hundred meters. Even an atmospheric diving suit can't go that far down."

Selena said, "We'll use an ROV to survey the site. If we find something we need to examine, Jeff has a DSV that can reach two thousand meters."

"A Deep Submergence Vehicle? This guy must be rolling in dough."

"I told you he was wealthy," Selena said. "It's a Pisces class, built in British Columbia. The NOOA has two of them."

"Those ruins are twenty-four hundred feet down," Nick said. "I don't like the idea of you going down there. What if something happens?"

"We won't be going deep enough to test the limit."

"Unless something happens."

"It's the only way if something has to be studied."

"I still don't like it," Nick said.

"It might not be necessary. It depends on what we find with the ROV."

"Those ruins are pretty spread out. It's going to take time to search through them."

Lamont looked at his watch. "It's 1600. We're not going to get down there today."

"Let's get the gear squared away," Ronnie said.

"While you do that, I'll go talk to Sexton," Nick said.

He headed back up to the bridge and found Sexton studying the sonar scans.

"Look at this."

Sexton pointed at a progression of shapes on the ocean floor below. The shapes ended in a ragged line. After that there was only blackness.

"Whatever's down there is right on the edge of the abyssal plain," Sexton said. "The depth of the ruins is consistent at about eight hundred meters up to that point. At the edge there's a sharp drop off. After that, it's a long way down."

"Selena says you have a DSV that can go deep."

"That's right. We have a Pisces class two-man submersible that can reach two thousand meters. Are you thinking of going down there?"

"I don't know yet. It depends on what we find tomorrow. I'd like you to send down an ROV so we could take a look. We'll decide what to do after that."

"I've got the perfect unit for the job. Camera, lights and small enough to get into some tight places."

Nick smiled in spite of himself. Sexton's enthusiasm was infectious. Nick saw why Selena had been attracted to him. He was hard not to like.

The thought didn't help much.

CHAPTER 36

The windows of the R/V *Tolstoy*'s bridge looked out from five stories above the main deck. The view would have been spectacular, if there had been anything to see except the sun reflecting off an empty ocean. Valentina watched water foam past the bow and wished she were someplace where she didn't have to deal with Katerina Rostov. The two women stood on the bridge, waiting for the captain to complete a calculation.

"At our present rate of speed we will reach the coordinates you specified about 0300 tomorrow," he said.

"We should have gotten there sooner," Katerina said. "If you had left when ordered, we would be there now."

Captain Vorochenko controlled his temper. It was necessary to be careful around the security services, even though his word was law on the *Tolstoy*. Once they returned to port, he was just another civilian.

"We're making the highest speed possible, Major. I can't change the laws of physics."

"We lost needless time leaving Egypt."

"This isn't a pleasure craft. We had to complete refueling and transfer some personnel off the ship because of your security concerns. If we were slow leaving port, it was a result of the demands you placed upon me."

"Your attitude will be noted, *Captain*."

Rostov's voice said there would be consequences from Vorochenko's attitude, none of them good. She turned and stalked out of the bridge.

In a conversational tone Valentina said, "She walks like she has a stick up her ass, doesn't she?" Vorochenko looked at her with surprise.

"Do not worry, Captain. I am in charge of this expedition, not her. Whatever she reports will be countermanded. You are doing your best. That is all that is needed."

"What is her problem?"

"What is always the problem with people like her? She thinks the world should bend to her will. Even laws of physics."

"Can you tell me why I'm burning up my engines to get to an empty spot in the ocean?"

"Not an empty spot, not below the surface. All you need to know right now is that the Americans are there ahead of us and that there's something on the ocean floor that may be vital to our national security."

"Please excuse my curiosity."

Valentina wanted the captain on her side if an accident happened to Rostov. It wouldn't be that difficult. The FSB major had started criticizing Vorochenko the moment she'd boarded his ship.

"As I said, Captain, do not worry. I suggest you make sure your submersibles are ready to go at short notice."

"As you wish, Major."

Valentina left the bridge and walked aft until she reached the stairs leading down to the lower decks. She saw Rostov two decks down, talking with one of the Spetsnaz divers who'd come on board with her, a sergeant named Nikita Spassky. Valentina had known a man named Nikita once. He'd made the mistake of thinking she was another woman he could force to have sex with him and ended up in an emergency room. Valentina had decided that anyone named Nikita was to be avoided. The muscular diver was no exception.

He complicates things, she thought. *Harder to create an accident with the divers around. That one always seems to be with her.*

Vysotsky had been clear. If Katerina Rostov became a problem, eliminate her. As far as Valentina was concerned Rostov was already a problem, if for no other reason than because she was arrogant and abrasive.

At that moment Rostov looked up at her. The eyes of the two women locked. Rostov's lips curled down. She turned back to her companion.

If looks could kill one of us would be dead now, Valentina thought.

By the time she reached the lower deck Rostov and the diver had disappeared inside. Valentina made her way to the stern and leaned against the railing, watching the wake trail out behind the ship. The ship's cook appeared with a pail of slops. He nodded at her and dumped the slops over the side. The garbage spread out behind the ship on the surface of the water.

There were always seagulls circling above, tracking the ship. They dove for the feast, striking the water and lifting into the air with whatever they had seized.

I wonder what it would be like to be like one of those birds, Valentina thought. *Sailing on the wind over the ocean, wherever I wanted to go.*

As she watched, two of the gulls turned on one another, fighting over a scrap.

Maybe not. It doesn't look like it's much different from being human.

She turned to go back to her cabin and saw Rostov coming out onto the deck. Nikita was right behind her. He moved away to the port railing. Rostov continued toward the stern.

She looks flushed, Valentina thought. *I'll bet she's been screwing Nikita in there.*

"Major Antipov."

"Major Rostov."

"If this fool of a captain is correct in his figures, we will reach our target tomorrow. We need to talk about how to proceed."

"Let me guess," Valentina said. "You have a plan."

Rostov looked away and said something inaudible.

"I'm sorry," Valentina said. "I didn't quite catch that. What did you say?"

"It doesn't matter. Look, we don't like each other, but we have to work together."

"For the good of the *Rodina*?"

"Exactly. What are your orders?"

"My orders? To observe. To find out what's down there, if anything. To monitor the Americans. I expect those are your orders as well."

"The Americans present a problem."

"And does your plan include them?"

"They must not be allowed to learn anything that threatens our security," Rostov said.

"What do you propose to do?"

"Nikita is highly skilled in underwater demolition. If they find anything, he will destroy their craft. Whatever they learn will vanish with the ship."

Rostov watched to see her reaction. Valentina gave no sign of what she was thinking and feeling.

My sister is on that ship, you bitch. And you know it.

"That could provoke serious repercussions," Valentina said. "Is Volkov foolish enough to risk the wrath of the Americans on mere suspicion?"

"You should be careful what you say, Antipov. Director Volkov has only the good of the Motherland at heart. Criticism of his decisions may reflect badly on you. Any attempts on your part to interfere could be seen as treason."

"Treason?"

"Do I have to mention your sister, the American spy?"

For a brief instant, Valentina imagined throwing Rostov over the side for the gulls to feed on. *Into the propellers would be good. The pieces would be smaller, easier for the birds to pick up.*

"I wouldn't be quick to make accusations if I were you," Valentina said. "For an officer to have an affair with an enlisted man is punishable by court-martial. Or had you forgotten that?"

"You dare to accuse me?"

"Come on, Rostov. Anyone can see you're fucking that gorilla. What's his name? Spassky? So drop the threats and try to be professional."

Rostov made an effort to control herself. "Perhaps such extreme measures with the Americans will not be necessary."

"I'm glad to hear it," Valentina said.

"We will make an initial survey with the remote vehicle. I assume you agree to that?"

"Yes. What else do you have in mind?"

"Whatever happens next depends on what we find."

"It would be wise to avoid a confrontation with the Americans in the water. Even someone as experienced as Sergeant Spassky can get into trouble."

Rostov looked at Valentina, wondering if what she had said was a veiled threat.

"I'm sure Spassky can take care of himself. I want to know if we have an agreement to make this go smoothly."

"We are in agreement about one important thing," Valentina said.

"Yes?"

"If there's anything in those ruins that will help our country, we will bring it back."

CHAPTER 37

"We have company," Selena said.

She pointed at a ship that had come up during the night and anchored a few hundred yards away.

Nick raised a pair of binoculars to his eyes and read the name on the bow.

"That's the Russian ship we saw in Egypt."

"What do you think she's doing here?" Lamont said.

"Same thing we are."

Nick watched people moving around on deck.

"Ronnie, where's that camera with the telephoto lens?"

"In the cabin." He looked over at the Russian ship. "I'll go get it."

"Thanks."

Ronnie came back with the camera and handed it to Nick. He focused the powerful lens on a group of people standing near the Stern. A dark-haired woman came on deck.

Shit, Nick thought. *That's Selena's sister. What's she doing out here?*

Valentina walked over to the group. One of them turned around and Nick recognized the woman who had tried to kidnap Selena in the hotel. He didn't recognize any of the others. He took several pictures of the group and of the ship to send off to Harker later.

"There's something you need to know," Nick said to Selena.

"What's wrong?"

"Your sister is on that ship."

"Valentina? Where?"

Nick handed the camera and lens over to Selena. He pointed at the cluster of people on the aft deck of the *Tolstoy*.

"She's in that group at the stern, talking to the only other woman on deck. That's the one who tried to grab you."

Selena looked through the lens.

"Shit."

"Yeah, that's what I thought."

"You think Valentina is working with her?"

"Looks that way."

"How did the Russians know we're here?"

"We had to get out of Cairo in a hurry. Maybe they found your notes."

"That would explain it. Everything was on my computer. But it doesn't explain why Valentina is here."

The ship was getting ready for the day. Dress code on the *Sexton's Dream* was casual. The crew was relaxed, joking with each other as they went about their tasks. Sexton ran a happy ship.

"We'll be ready to go right after chow," Nick said. "Sexton has an ROV he says is perfect for the job."

"How many ROVs does he have?" Lamont asked.

"Two, I think. Plus the DSV. "

"Jeffrey's a serious researcher," Selena said.

"Mmm." Nick emptied his cup.

An hour and a half later, two crewmen swung the ROV over the side with an articulated arm and lowered it into the water. It bobbed on the surface, half submerged. A fiber-optic tether to control the vehicle led back to a caged feed on the deck.

The body of the rover was made of high density orange-colored plastic, enclosed in a frame of sled-like tubing. The unit was small, about three feet long by two and a half wide. Thrusters on either end were powered by a large twenty-four volt battery. An additional vertical thruster added more maneuverability. LED lights in front provided illumination for the camera.

Nick looked over at the *Tolstoy*. He counted three pairs of binoculars focused on what they were doing.

"Time to go to the communications room," he said.

The communications room was where the control console and monitors for the ROV were located. The operator was an athletic-looking woman with dark brown hair, one of the ship's officers. She'd dressed in shorts and a T-shirt. Nick read what was written on the shirt.

"I used to be schizophrenic but we're so much better now."

Her console had dual joysticks and a monitor displaying the image from the rover's camera. Everything the camera saw would be recorded in full color, high definition video. At the moment the monitor showed water breaking over the camera as the ROV bobbed on the surface. The operator could manipulate two arms with mechanical fingers that were capable of picking up a coin from the ocean floor.

"This is Vicki," Sexton said.

Vicki flashed a smile and went back to her console.

"Ready to go look for a myth?"

"Let's do it," Nick said.

Sexton turned to Vicki. "Everything looking good?"

"Everything is a go. All systems functioning."

"Send her down."

"Down, aye."

Vicki took hold of the joysticks. The image on the monitor changed as the rover sank beneath the surface. A vertical display on the side of the screen showed battery charge, speed, depth, time remaining, external pressure and other indicators of the health of the vehicle.

Nick and the others watched as the rover descended.

"Twenty meters. All systems normal."

Gradually the light faded.

"Thirty meters," Vicki said. "Turning on the lights."

She touched a switch and bright streams of light poured out into the growing darkness. A large shape swam past the camera and was gone.

"What was that?" Ronnie asked.

"Shark," Sexton said. "Lots of them out here."

Selena and Lamont looked at each other.

"I hate sharks," Lamont said.

"Forty meters."

The depth chart kept changing as the robot sank deeper into the ocean and total darkness. It passed seven hundred and eighty meters. Bits of debris floated past the camera's eye.

"Getting close," Nick said.

Vicki adjusted the speed, slowing the vehicle.

"She'd be a good drone operator," Lamont said.

"She was one," Sexton said. "Vicki did a tour in the Air Force, most of it at Nellis in Nevada. Running Reapers over Afghanistan and Iraq."

"This is more fun," Vicki said. "Whoa, look at that."

She brought the ROV to a stop, holding position with delicate adjustments to the thrusters. The depth gauge read eight hundred and two meters.

Peering at them out of the blackness was a gigantic, stone face.

"Doesn't look like he's having a good day," Lamont said to Ronnie.

"You can't blame him. How would you like to spend five or ten thousand years underwater?"

"That head must be thirty feet tall," Selena said. "It looks like it's carved out of one solid piece of stone."

"Could be part of a statue," Lamont said.

Sexton put his hand on Vicki's chair. "Take a look to the left. I saw something as you moved in."

Vicki adjusted the joysticks and the ROV swiveled to the left. The lights revealed a second stone head rising out of the seabed, this one canted at an angle. The heads bordered a gap in a high wall.

"Wow," Ronnie said.

"If those are statues, everything will be under a hell of a lot of muck and silt," Nick said. "Not good for finding what we're looking for."

"Are you looking for something specific?" Vicki asked.

Selena said, "It might not have been a natural disaster that destroyed Atlantis. It's possible the people that lived here caused it. We're looking for something to tell us what happened."

It was partly true.

"Keep going left," Sexton said.

A narrow plume of white vapor rose from the seabed in front of the wall. It disappeared above the camera's field of view.

"What's that?" Selena asked.

Sexton said, "It's a sign of volcanic activity."

As the robot continued along the wall they saw two more of the vapor plumes.

"Several major tectonic plates come together in this part of the Atlantic. It's always active here."

"Do those plumes mean there's going to an eruption?"

"Not necessarily, but it's not a good sign."

The robot moved left, following the wall until it came to a sudden end where the seabed dropped sharply away. The robot had reached the abyss marking the boundary of the ruins.

Lamont said, "It looks like the earth opened up under them."

"That slope drops away for thousands of meters," Sexton said.

Nick said, "Go back to the heads. They look like they make the sides of a gate. Let's see what's on the other side of the wall."

The robot turned back through the water and reached the stone heads. Vicki guided it through the opening. The lights revealed the shapes of ruined buildings rising from the silt and mud. They spotted more of the vapor plumes.

"Everything's half buried," Ronnie said.

"Not everything," Vicki said. "There's something big ahead."

The rover came to a broad wall of dark stone crusted with sea growth, slanting up toward the surface far above.

"What is it?" Ronnie asked.

Under Vicki's control, the robot followed the slope up. As they neared the top it became evident the structure was a pyramid.

"I'll be damned," Sexton said.

The top of the pyramid was three hundred feet above the seafloor. A large, square opening at the peak gaped out at them. Long strands of seaweed drifted in lazy patterns about the opening.

"This is eerie," Selena said. "It's like finding Egypt underwater. These people had to be far advanced to build that."

"Can you get the robot through that opening?" Nick asked.

"Let me get closer."

Vicki brought the robot up to the opening. The lights revealed nothing from the outside.

"It will fit. We need to be careful, though. It would be easy to get trapped in there."

"Go ahead and take her in," Sexton said.

With a touch at the controls, the robot moved slowly into the interior of the pyramid . A school of odd looking fish swam past the camera and out through the opening. As the robot moved around they saw three more openings like the one they had come through, one on each of the four sides. It was a kind of room. There was a floor covered with silt. Nothing else could be seen but a wide, black shaft in the middle of the floor.

"That's weird," Lamont said.

"Follow that down, Vick."

"You're the boss."

The ROV tilted and headed down into darkness. Two hundred and fifty feet down, the robot emerged into a large chamber at the bottom of the pyramid. Countless centuries of sea muck covered the pyramid floor.

Vicki moved the robot around the room, trying not to kick up debris with the thrusters. Even so, a fine mist of silt began to cloud the water, limiting visibility. It was dreamlike, the walls shifting in and out of focus. Unlike the outside of the pyramid, the interior walls were free of growth.

"That's odd," Sexton said. "Why isn't anything growing inside?"

Selena touched Vicki's shoulder. "Can you hold the robot right there without stirring up more silt?"

"I'll try."

The robot paused as Vicki held it in position. Slowly the water cleared enough to see what Selena was looking at. The inner wall of the pyramid was covered with the writing she'd named Linear D.

"Is the camera recording this?"

"Yes, ma'am."

Selena said, "This is incredible."

"What does it say?" Nick asked.

"It's like the columns and the tablet. These people seem to have been obsessed with their achievements and the greatness of their empire. At first glance it's a history of their expansion into North Africa. At least I think it's about North Africa. Make sure we get everything on that wall."

Vicki worked the robot back and forth until everything had been caught on tape.

"What about the other walls?" Nick said.

"I'll look," Vicki said.

For the next forty-five minutes they recorded the other walls of the pyramid on video. Each wall was covered with writing to a height of about twenty feet, interrupted by blank squares set at regular intervals. The lower lines of writing were obscured by the buildup of silt and muck.

"What do you think those squares were?" Lamont asked.

"Probably paintings," Selena said. "Pictures to go along with the story. Anything like that would've been gone a long time ago."

"We need to bring the robot up," Vicki said. "The battery is running low."

"We have enough pictures for now," Selena said.

"Bring her home, Vicki," Sexton said.

The robot turned and started up toward the shaft leading to the peak of the pyramid. Sudden bright light blinded the camera. The image tilted crazily and went dark. Vicki worked the controls on the console with no result.

"I've lost her. The robot's not responding. Something hit the unit."

Nick's face was tight and angry.

"I'll bet I know what it was," he said.

"Yeah," Ronnie said. "The Russians."

CHAPTER 38

The heat of the day had not yet begun and the patio doors of Elizabeth's office were open to the early morning. She poured a cup of coffee and went outside, where Stephanie sat at a shaded patio table. For the moment it was a pleasant morning in the Virginia countryside, the kind of morning when Elizabeth could pretend there was nothing more important to worry about than what she would have for lunch.

"I wonder what they're going to find down there," Stephanie said as Elizabeth sat down.

"The whole thing is hard to believe, isn't it? People have been arguing about the existence of Atlantis ever since Plato wrote about it."

"I wouldn't be surprised if they kept on arguing. A lot of experts are going to look pretty foolish if it really is Atlantis. They aren't going to want to believe it, even in the face of hard evidence."

"I've never understood why people are like that." Elizabeth sipped her coffee. "I can understand resisting change. Nobody really likes change. But when evidence smacks you in the face and you choose to ignore it, that's just stupidity."

"Nobody said humans were logical or sensible. All you have to do is look at Congress."

Elizabeth choked on her coffee, trying not to laugh.

Her satellite phone signaled Nick was calling.

"Good morning, Nick."

"We have a problem. The Russians showed up."

Elizabeth looked over at Stephanie. She activated the speaker.

"I was afraid that would happen."

"Do you have a satellite on us?"

"The next pass is in three hours from now. I can have a drone there before that. Is it a Federation warship?"

"No, it's a research vessel like ours, only bigger. There's already trouble. They knocked out one of our ROVs when it was underwater. I want eyes on us in case they decide to play rough."

"I'll task a drone after we're done talking. What have you found so far?"

"A ruined city, twenty-four hundred feet down. There's a pyramid in the middle of it. That's where we lost the robot. We've got footage of the interior. The walls are covered with writing, the same language that's on the pillar and the French tablet. Selena says it looks like a history of some sort. It will be a while before she has a translation."

"Any sign of an archive?"

"Not unless it's what's written on those walls. Everything's under silt and debris."

"What's your plan now?"

"We're going to send another ROV down. Sexton wants to recover his unit. We'll put someone in the water in case the Russians decide to go after this one too. They're not going to get away with it again."

"Be careful, Nick. This could turn into a major incident."

"There's more. Selena's sister is on that ship. So is the woman who shot at me in Egypt."

"That's not good," Elizabeth said. A headache started, a dull ache behind her left eye.

"I took pictures of everyone that was on deck. I'll send them to Steph when we're done talking. Might be useful."

"Brief me as soon as you know anything else."

"Copy that. Out."

Stephanie's phone chimed as Nick's pictures came through.

"I'll get these printed out."

Stephanie picked up her coffee and went inside. Elizabeth sat for a while longer, trying to hold on to the morning calm. After a few minutes she gave up and went inside.

For the next hour she focused on the morning's intelligence briefs, making comments for the president's consideration. Today was one of those days when the actions of so-called allies created almost as many problems as enemies. Elizabeth never ceased to be amazed at how so many incompetent and corrupt leaders reached positions of power.

Her father would have put it down to human nature. He'd been a judge in Western Colorado, where Elizabeth had grown up. More than once he'd challenged her perception of how life ought to be. Sometimes it had been uncomfortable, but it had helped make her the person she was today.

Before President Rice asked her to head up the Project, Elizabeth had worked in the Justice Department. At one point she'd been assigned to the 9/11 task force. After a few months she'd noticed a pattern about the investigation. Key pieces of information were being suppressed and kept from the public. When she went to her supervisor to point it out, he'd told her not to make waves. When she'd insisted, he'd told her to take a week off and think about it.

She'd gone home, angry and frustrated, venting her frustration to her father.

What do you want to do about it? he'd asked.

This investigation is being manipulated. I've seen evidence that proves the public narrative isn't what really happened.

You think there's a cover-up? Her father had taken out his pipe and begun filling it with tobacco.

It's hard to see any other explanation. The evidence just doesn't add up. Not only that, there was plenty of intelligence pointing to an imminent attack. It looks like it might have been deliberately ignored.

The judge lit his pipe and took several puffs. The sweet aroma of cured Turkish tobacco drifted across the porch where they sat.

Suppose you were able to make this information public. What do you think would happen?

I'm not sure anyone would believe me, Elizabeth had said.

And if they did?

It would cause big problems. If I'm right, this wasn't only a terrorist attack. Whoever's responsible should be held to account.

Let's say you're right, the judge had said. *If it's what you say it is, the people behind it aren't going to let anyone change what you call the narrative.*

I'm not afraid of them.

You ought to be. If you really want to do something about it, you'll have to take a different approach.

What approach?

In a way, you're already doing it. In the 1920s the American Communists talked about boring from within to bring change. They were right about that, even though they were wrong about everything else.

Her father had held up his pipe.

Democracy is like this pipe, he'd said. *We have to pay attention if we want to keep it burning. It requires care. If you want to make a difference, you're not going to get it by playing Don Quixote against the system. It's too well-developed and too powerful. You have to bore from within.*

It doesn't feel right to keep silent, Elizabeth had said.

That's your choice. Just be careful you don't take yourself out of the game. You can't play if you're not on the field.

When she'd returned to Washington, she'd kept asking uncomfortable questions. Two months later she was transferred to an endless RICO investigation. Her career had been shunted into a dead-end. Then Rice had called.

Stephanie came into the room, breaking Elizabeth's reverie. She had a folder under her arm.

"I printed and enlarged Nick's pictures. I got hits when I ran them through the facial identification program."

She laid the photographs out on Elizabeth's desk.

Selena's sister was in several of the shots. It looked like she was arguing with another woman. Two large men stood nearby.

"The woman with Selena's sister is an FSB officer named Rostov," Stephanie said. "She works directly under Volkov. He uses her as his personal attack dog. The two goons standing there are Russian Special Forces. They're from the Federation equivalent of our SEALS."

"Divers?"

"Seems logical."

"The Russians must know what's down there," Elizabeth said.

"Selena's sister is SVR. Why is she on a ship with someone from the FSB? Those two services don't cooperate worth a damn."

"It means Orlov has a hand in this. I know how Vysotsky thinks. He hates Volkov. He would never work with him unless ordered to do so. Orlov is playing some game."

"What do you think he's up to?" Stephanie asked.

"With Orlov you can't tell until after the fact. Whatever it is, that ship being there is bad news."

Elizabeth drummed her fingers on the desk.

"Are you going to take this to the president?" Stephanie asked.

"Not yet. I want pictures of what they found. I want Selena's translation of what they discovered. All we have now are underwater ruins and minor incidents. It's not enough."

"The Russians tried to kidnap Selena and kill Nick when they were in Egypt."

"Like I said, incidents. I need more before I can go to the White House. We need to know what that writing says."

"If I know Selena, she's working on it right now," Stephanie said.

"I'm sure she is."

"You need me for anything? I have a doctor's appointment."

"Is everything okay?"

"It's only a routine checkup. I'll be back in a couple of hours."

"Take your time."

"Thanks."

She left the room. Elizabeth leaned back in her chair and thought about how odd it was to be alone in the building during the day. Stephanie was always available for a talk over a cup of coffee. Aside from Stephanie and the team, there wasn't anyone else she could talk with.

During the day she was too busy with work to feel lonely. She loved interacting with the team. It was heady stuff to command the attention of the president. All of that was little consolation when she came home to her empty brownstone.

She thought about Clarence Hood. The trouble stirred up by the photograph was beginning to die down but a congressional inquiry was still a possibility, if for no other reason than to try and embarrass the president.

Maybe Clarence would like to have dinner this evening, she thought.

Elizabeth picked up her phone.

CHAPTER 39

By now Selena had a good grasp of the ancient language. She made rapid progress with the writing on the pyramid walls, working on the translation until it was past midnight. After a few hours of sleep, she went back to it. By morning she had a rough translation for most of one wall.

She sat with Nick in the wardroom, drinking coffee, a laptop open in front of her.

"When we found those murals in Tibet I thought nothing would top it," she said. "I thought no new find could possibly surpass it."

"Sounds like you've changed your mind," Nick said.

"What's down there changes world history. It's a record of a civilization everyone thought was a fable."

"So, it is Atlantis?"

"Yes. Only they didn't call it that, of course. Their word for it translates to 'us' or 'the people.' I don't know what's on those other walls but what I've already seen is enough to keep archaeologists and historians busy for years."

"Did you come across anything about an archive? Where it might be?"

"Not yet, unless that pyramid is it. But I found more about the stone that controlled the force they used to lift things. The Stone of the Gods."

"I still don't see how a stone could do anything like that."

"Modern technology uses stones. Diamond lasers, for example. They're powerful enough to cut through steel. Diamonds are a kind of stone."

"Yeah, but this is the twenty-first century. You know, electricity, microchips, things like that. Where did they get energy from?"

"However it worked, these people used it to lift blocks of stone weighing tons off the ground. Then they pushed them through the air and dropped them into place."

"That's hard to believe. Like everything else about this."

"These people might have built the pyramids in Egypt. The rulers used the same energy to get around. They rode on a kind of sled that floated above the ground."

"Mmm."

"Mmm? Is that all you have to say about it?"

"What do you expect me to say?"

"Oh, I don't know. Maybe 'wow, that's really something.' I just told you these people mastered gravity and all you can say is 'Mmm.'"

"Unless we can find out how they did it, it's a fairy tale," Nick said.

Selena looked at him and sighed. "There's a lot I haven't translated yet."

"While you've been doing this, Sexton is getting another ROV ready. He'll send it down after breakfast."

"What if the Russians interfere again?"

"Lamont has been talking with one of Sexton's divers. He was a SEAL, too. They're going to go over the side at the same time as the ROV. If the Russians try anything funny, those two will stop it from happening."

"I want to go down with them," Selena said.

"I thought you would but you've been up most of the night. You're tired and I need you up here. You're the only one who can work on the translation. We need to understand what else is on those walls."

Selena was about to argue. Then she said, "I know you're right. But I don't have to like it."

He looked at his watch. "Let's eat. It's going to be a long day."

A half hour later they were on deck, where Sexton was ready to launch the second ROV. He was going to try and retrieve the robot lost the day before.

Lamont and his new partner were suited up, ready to go over the side.

"This is Sam Heath," Lamont said. "He got out a few years before I did. We know a lot of the same people."

Sam had a broad Irish face, blue eyes and a shock of thick, red hair. He shook hands with Nick and Selena. His smile was genuine.

"Nice to meet you."

"Likewise," Nick said. "You know what you could be getting into?"

"You mean the Russians? They don't bother me."

"Do you want us to take out their robot if they send it down again?" Lamont asked. "We could cut the tether."

Nick nodded. "They called the game. Let's raise the stakes."

"What if they put men in the water?" Sam asked.

"Good question. It depends on what they do. Try to avoid a confrontation. If they come after you, protect yourself."

"That's what I wanted to hear," Sam said.

Sexton came over. "We're ready to go."

"Let's do it," Lamont said.

Across the way on the *Tolstoy*, Katerina Rostov studied the bustle of activity on board the *Sexton's Dream*. The two Spetsnaz divers stood next to her.

"They're getting ready to put men in the water," Rostov said. "Now they're lowering an ROV."

"What are your orders?" Spassky asked.

"We're launching our own unit. The Americans may try to sabotage it in retaliation for yesterday. You will prevent that from happening."

"We can only follow it down so far," Spassky said. "As we go deeper, we have less time."

"The same is true for them."

"What are the rules of engagement?"

"If they cause no trouble, ignore them."

"And if they do?"

"You are to prevent anything that will interfere with this mission by any means necessary. Is that clear?"

"You are not concerned about consequences if we have to kill them?"

"You have your orders, Sergeant."

CHAPTER 40

Lamont and Sam wore full face masks equipped with voice communication. They could talk to each other while they were underwater and to Nick on board *Sexton's Dream*. Both men wore closed-circuit rebreathers and wetsuits. There would be no telltale bubbles on the surface as they approached the Russian ship.

At twenty feet down there was plenty of light. The surface above was clear blue, the sun a halo glow scattering streams of light through the water. Lamont never tired of the world that existed below the surface of the sea. Most people never saw the true beauty of the ocean.

The Atlantic this far out from land teemed with life. The area was famed with sports fishermen for its abundance of trophy fish. Blue marlin, swordfish and giant bluefin tuna were common. Plenty of fish meant plenty of sharks, including hammerheads, short fin makos and a throwback called the six gill blunt nose. Hammerheads were usually not aggressive unless provoked. The others were. As far as Lamont was concerned, any kind of shark was bad news.

A hundred yards away, the long hull of the Russian ship formed a dark shape on the surface of the water.

"Comm check," Lamont said. "Sam, how do you read me?"

"Five by five."

"Nick, you copy?"

Nick's voice came back through the earpiece. "Five by five, amigo. The Russians are about to put their robot over the side."

"Copy that."

Lamont and Sam dropped down to forty feet and moved silently toward the Russian ship. Visibility was still excellent, the water clear. A school of silvery-blue wahoo swam by, slim and lethal looking, their sharp teeth and spiny ridges a reminder of a time long before humans walked the earth.

The Russian ROV was visible as it descended past the forty foot mark. The tether was a dark thread linking the machine to the ship above. The two men swam toward it. Lamont was equipped with a tool borrowed from the ship designed to cut through cable and chain. It would make short work of the tether. He was about to reach for it when his earpiece crackled.

"Company," Sam said.

He pointed toward the bow of the ship. Two suited figures were coming toward them.

"Armed. They've got APS assault rifles."

The semi automatic APS was a favorite of Russian underwater special forces, a unique piece of weapons engineering. It hadn't been easy to design a gun that could overcome the compressive effects of water against the moving parts of an automatic weapon, much less deliver a projectile with reasonable accuracy.

Water was eight hundred times denser than air. A man could stand a few feet in front of a conventional weapon fired underwater without danger. The APS used special cartridges and 5.66 mm steel bolts that could penetrate a diver's helmet or wetsuit with ease. It was most effective at a distance of twenty or thirty feet and reasonably accurate. The Russians had even designed a cartridge with a rocket assist to give it more speed and penetrating power.

Lamont and Sam carried Heckler and Koch P11 underwater pistols. The pistols had five chambers and fired steel darts a little less than four inches long. The P11 had a greater range than the APS but its accuracy was poor. Both kinds of weapons were better than knives or spear guns for underwater combat.

Nick's voice sounded over the comm link. "Two divers in the water."

"We see them," Lamont said. "They're armed."

"Break off," Nick said. "It's not worth it."

"Copy," Lamont said. "Sam, break it off."

The Russian in the lead raised his weapon and fired while he was still fifty feet away. Steel bolts ripped through the water, too fast for the eye to see, leaving a brief disturbance behind.

"Too late," Sam said.

On deck, Nick had the comm link on speaker.

"Lamont, what's happening?"

Selena had gone to her cabin for her notes. She came out on deck and went over to where Nick was standing.

"What's going on?"

"Trouble. Lamont, come in."

Below the surface, Lamont drew his pistol and fired at one of the Russian divers. The round missed. The man started to bring his APS around. Water resistance against the large, flat magazine and receiver slowed the movement. Lamont fired again. The Russian clutched his shoulder and dropped his rifle. Blood spread in the water, a soft, dark cloud.

The other Russian emptied his magazine at them. Steel bolts shattered Sam's face mask. His arms flew wide and he went limp. His body sank away toward the depths below.

Rage drove Lamont toward the Russian, firing his pistol as he swam. All of the three rounds he had left missed. The P11 came pre-loaded from the factory. Even if there'd been time, he couldn't have loaded it again. He dropped the pistol and drew his knife. The Russian let go of his empty rifle and reached for his own knife. Lamont slashed out, opening a deep cut. More blood seeped into the water.

The Russian wasn't out of the fight. He lunged forward, trying for a gut thrust. Lamont twisted away but the blade sliced through his suit and into his arm. His own blood mixed with the Russian's. Lamont looked into the man's face and saw sudden fear. He sensed a shadow behind him.

Shark!

A sudden blow knocked him to the side. The shark slammed into the Russian, taking him with wide open jaws. The ugly, pointed teeth were close enough for Lamont to touch as the monster went by. The man thrashed in helpless agony as the shark swam away with him. The water was suddenly black with blood

The diver Lamont had wounded was swimming away as fast as he could. A second shark appeared, a vision from hell. It zeroed in on the wounded Russian, clamped it's terrible teeth around his legs and dragged him away.

The fight was over.

"Nick, it's bad. Sam's dead. Sharks and I'm wounded. Get ready to pull me out."

"Copy."

Lamont fumbled for a packet of shark repellent. The chemicals were supposed to smell like a dead shark and the live ones didn't like it. He ripped open the package, released the chemicals and started for the surface. Hoping they worked. Hoping no more sharks appeared. A thin trail of blood streamed behind him.

On deck, Sexton began giving orders.

"Get the zodiac in the water. He's not far from the Russian ship."

"Lamont," Nick said, "we're putting a boat in the water. Stay cool."

"Copy."

Lamont had been more than forty feet down but it was his first dive of the day and he didn't need to make a decompression stop. There wouldn't have been time for one anyway, not with sharks nearby. He still had his knife, but his arm was weakening.

He looked down. More sharks circled below. One of them started for him. He was nearing the surface but the shark was closer. He turned to face it.

Only one chance.

Four blue-gray shapes shot through the water and passed by him. They attacked the pursuing shark.

Dolphins. They're Dolphins...

Lamont broke the surface near the *Tolstoy*. The Russians were letting a boat down into the water. The railing was lined with people watching. He saw Selena's sister. Lamont swiveled and saw the zodiac from *Sexton's Dream* racing toward him.

A man appeared at the railing of the Russian ship with a bull horn.

"We are sending someone to assist you."

Lamont raised his good arm and gave them a middle finger.

CHAPTER 41

Nick stopped the bleeding with a temporary dressing.

"Hang in there. We're almost back to the ship."

"Heath is dead." Lamont said. "The Russians shot him. A shark got the bastard."

"Yeah."

They reached the ship and got Lamont on board. The Dolphins had followed the zodiac back to the ship. Now they circled once around *Sexton's Dream* and disappeared.

Nick paced the deck.

"We didn't need this." He looked at the *Tolstoy*.

"I don't know who's running things over there, but they're nuts to try a stunt like this," Ronnie said

"What are we going to do about it?" Selena asked.

"There isn't much we can do," Nick said, "short of starting a war."

"Another minor incident? Is that how we're going to treat it? First they trash our rover. Now one of Jeff's crew is dead."

"What would you have me do? Tell your pal to ram them? Plant explosives and blow them out of the water?"

"That sounds like a good idea."

"You used to have second thoughts about what we do. When did you get so blood thirsty?"

"You have to agree it has a certain appeal."

"Yes, but you know I can't do that."

"I know you can't sink them. Besides, Valentina is on that boat. How about something less extreme? Something to disable them, like a small explosion."

Ronnie said, "We need to stop them messing with us."

"I can't ask Sexton to put another one of his crew in harm's way. Lamont's out of commission."

Selena raised her hand. "I can do it."

"You're not trained in underwater demolition. It has to be me or Ronnie. Besides, Harker would never authorize it."

"She doesn't have to know about it. How hard can it be to plant something on the hull that goes boom?"

"You're serious."

"Damn right I am. These people think they can get away with anything. We have to respond and I'm the best one to do it. We can't get near on the surface without being spotted and that means going deep. Neither one of you has the experience I do when it comes to diving."

"Ronnie and I both have underwater training."

"I want to do this. Those people over there tried to kidnap me. I was tasered."

"This isn't about getting even," Nick said.

"No? Then think of it as a preemptive move to prevent further interference with the mission."

In spite of himself, Nick smiled. "A small explosion, you said."

"That's right." Selena nodded. "Enough to give them something to think about. To keep them busy while we finish up."

"I can show her what to do," Ronnie said.

"You think this is a good idea, Lamont?"

"I almost bought it down there. Yeah, I think it's a good idea. It'll teach them a lesson."

"Harker will have a cow when she finds out."

Selena smiled at him. "Like I said, she doesn't have to know about it. Remember that old saying about forgiveness and permission?"

"You know they're going to keep screwing things up," Ronnie said. "I've got C4 and detonators in our kit. It won't take long to make up a charge."

Nick was quiet for a few seconds. "All right, Ronnie, go ahead."

"Right away, Kemo Sabe."

"I still don't know what that means."

"And you still don't want to know."

"I hope I don't regret this," Nick said.

Ronnie put together a charge and scrounged a magnet from the ship's stores. He taped it to the package. Once Selena got close enough to place the charge, the magnet would hold it on the hull of the Russian ship.

Two hours later she was getting ready to go in. Sexton came over to the group. He seemed angry.

"Going for a swim?" he said to her. "In a rebreather?"

"Only for a short reconnaissance. To make sure they don't have anyone in the water."

"Sam was a friend of mine. If I'd known you were going to put my crew at risk, I never would've agreed to do this. What the hell are you people up to? I never wanted to deal with this crap again, that's why I got out."

Nick said, "We didn't know the Russians would show up. I'm sorry about Sam, I really am. He seemed like a nice guy. But it's done."

"You're sorry. So am I. We're heading back to port."

"Look, I understand you're pissed off. Hold off and I'll fill you in on the mission. If you still want to leave after that, that's your option."

"Fair enough. But if I don't like what I hear, we're leaving."

He stalked away.

"Harker won't like telling him why we're here," Ronnie said.

"You heard what he said. If I don't tell him, he's pulling the plug. We don't have a choice."

"I need to go," Selena said. "While there's still light."

"Make sure you set that timer right," Ronnie said. "If it goes off and you're nearby in the water..." He left the sentence unfinished.

"Don't worry."

She slipped into the water on the far side of the ship, out of sight of the Russians. The afternoon light still gave some visibility below the surface. She dropped down to sixty feet, checking her dive calculator, tracking her time and depth.

She neared the *Tolstoy*, watching for divers. There was no one about. The sharks were gone. There was no sign of the bloody events of the morning.

Selena came up under the vessel and made her way aft. The tether to the Russian ROV formed a dark line disappearing into the depths below. Two enormous, silent propellers protruded into the water. She placed the charge and set the timer for forty minutes. It would give her more than enough time to return to the boat. There was no rush. The Russians had no idea she was there.

"Where'd you put the charge?" Ronnie asked when she was back on board.

"Right where the props come out of the hull. It should damage the shafts. Might even blow the tether on their robot."

Sexton passed by and came back to them. "Why are you all standing here?"

"We're waiting for the sunset," Ronnie said. "I was kind of hoping for the green flash."

"It's half an hour till the sun goes down."

No one said anything. Sexton shook his head.

"Meet me in the wardroom in fifteen minutes."

"Hey, Skipper," a crewman called.

"Coming." Sexton walked away.

Nick looked at his watch. "Any time now. You're sure you set the detonator the right way?"

"It's not rocket science, Nick. Yes, I'm sure."

The explosion, when it came, sent a tall fountain of water into the air. The sound echoed across the flat sea separating the two ships. The Tolstoy shuddered in the water.

"I might've used a little too much C4," Ronnie said.

CHAPTER 42

"What did you do to their ship?" Sexton asked Selena. "She's down some by the stern. They've got the pumps going."

"We wanted to stop them from harassing us."

"You've changed, Selena. I never would've figured you for something like this."

She shrugged. "Stuff happens."

Sexton looked at her as though she were a stranger.

Nick said, "I'm going to tell you why we're here."

Sexton listened while Nick filled him in.

"I don't believe this. You really think these people had something like antigravity? You're trying to find a record of what it was? What they used to control it?"

"That's about it."

"That's crazy."

"No more crazy than those ruins down there that aren't supposed to exist," Nick said. "The Russians don't think it's crazy. That's one of the reasons we have to follow up. What if it isn't crazy and the Russians find what we're looking for? We have to find it first. It's a matter of national security."

"I'm getting damn tired of hearing that phrase tossed around," Sexton said. "The politicians love it."

"Do I have to point out that I'm not a politician?"

Selena spoke up. "Jeff, I know you want to get out of here and I don't blame you. At least stay until I finish translating what's on those pyramid walls."

"I don't want any more surprises."

Nick held up his hand. "No more surprises. I promise."

"One more day. Then I'm leaving."

Nick went back to his cabin and called Harker to tell her what had happened. He got to the part about disabling the *Tolstoy.*

"You did what?" Harker said.

"We didn't sink them," Nick said.

The satellite connection was spotty, crackling with atmospherics.

"What didn't you think?"

"I said we didn't sink them."

"Oh, that makes me feel so much better," Harker said. "I can't wait until the president calls me up and asks me why I attacked a peaceful civilian research vessel belonging to the Federation."

"I don't think he's going to hear anything about it," Nick said. "They attacked us, not the other way around. Lamont almost died. One of Sexton's crew is dead and he was a civilian. If they make waves it's going to bounce back on them."

"Two of their people are dead."

Elizabeth thought she could hear Nick shrug on the other end of the connection.

"Like I said, they attacked us. They got more than they bargained for. I can't see how they'd want to turn this into an incident. It's to their advantage to keep quiet."

"You'd better be right."

Nick waited.

Elizabeth said, "All right, we'll move on. What's your plan now?"

"Sexton says there's an alert about seismic activity. The ruins are crawling with vapor columns that indicate something's happening down there. The city sits on the edge of a precipice and an undersea quake might finish the job. Selena wants to take one more look tomorrow for that archive. After that we're heading back to port."

"I don't want any more trouble with the Russians."

"We never wanted trouble in the first place. If they don't provoke us there won't be any more problems. There's one other thing you need to know."

Elizabeth began tapping her fingers on her desktop.

"I had to let Sexton it on what we're looking for. He was pretty ticked off about losing one of his people and ready to haul anchor. I didn't have any other option."

"Right now that's the least of my worries," Elizabeth said. "He signed the secrecy agreement."

"He's okay. You don't have to be concerned."

"Finish up and get out of there. The Russians may not turn it into an incident but they might retaliate. If you end up on the bottom of the ocean there's not much I can do about it."

"Thanks for the encouraging words."

"I want regular updates. That's all, Nick."

Elizabeth broke the connection.

Nick put his phone away and went up on deck. The others were waiting for him.

"I talked to Harker."

"What did she say?" Ronnie asked.

"She wasn't happy. She wants us out of here and she's worried about the Russians."

"She has a point."

"They won't try anything else if they're smart. Selena, where are you with that translation?

"I'm working on the last panel we photographed," Selena said. "I should have it done soon."

CHAPTER 43

The next morning there was a memorial service for Heath. The mood on the ship was somber, a far cry from the day before when people were joking and laughing as they worked.

Afterward Ronnie, Lamont and Nick stood aft by the port rail. Selena was below, finishing up her notes. The Russian ship was down by the stern but she wasn't sinking. They could hear the sound of the pumps keeping her afloat.

"Glad you're okay," Nick said.

"Those dolphins saved my ass. It was shark city down there. One of them thought I was lunch."

"I'd heard stories about dolphins protecting swimmers. Researchers say that's all they are, stories."

"Yeah, well, if one of those researchers had been down there he'd change his mind pretty quick."

"What's next?" Ronnie asked.

"After Sexton recovers his robot we'll make one more video run through the ruins. Then we're done."

Lamont looked over at the *Tolstoy*. "Too bad we couldn't sink her."

"At least they're too busy staying afloat to bother us."

They watched as Sexton's crew lowered the second ROV into the water. A minute later it disappeared under the surface.

Selena came over to them, excited. "I've found it."

"What? The archive?"

"Yes."

"Let's go inside," Nick said. "I want Harker to hear this."

The small cabin felt stuffy with all of them in it at the same time. Nick called Harker and put her on the speaker.

"Give me some good news, Nick."

"Selena thinks she's found the archive. I'm going to let her tell you about it."

"Hello, Elizabeth."

"You found the archive?"

"I found out where it is. The location was written on the wall of the pyramid."

"Is it down there in the ruins?"

"No. It's on the mainland."

"Where is it?"

She had her laptop open to her notes. "I'll read what was on the wall. It's the key."

In the green land where the Great River flows to the sea, we set the lion to guard for eternity the record of our people.

"That doesn't tell us much," Elizabeth said. "It could be anywhere."

"It's in Egypt," Selena said. "The Great River is the Nile."

"Why Egypt?"

"If I'm right, the lion that guards the secrets is the Sphinx. The archive is buried under it or nearby."

"There's nothing but sand around the Sphinx," Lamont said.

"It's on the west bank of the Nile. At one time the river flowed right by it. Before Egypt was desert it used to be green."

"Not for a hell of a long time."

Elizabeth listened as they talked.

"We're talking about a long time. Thousands of years ago, before the pharaohs ruled Egypt."

"I thought one of them built the Sphinx," Ronnie said.

"Not everyone agrees on that. There are some archaeologists who think the Pharaoh's face was added long after the Sphinx was constructed."

"Why would they think that?"

"Khufu is supposed to have commissioned the Sphinx at the same time as the great pyramid. The face is supposed to be his. But there's an account from the seventh century BCE that says when Khufu first saw it, the Sphinx was buried up to its head in sand."

"That doesn't make it thousands of years older."

"The Sphinx is built of limestone. It shows erosion caused by heavy rains. It hasn't rained hard enough to do that in Egypt for ten thousand years. Maybe longer. Suggestions the Sphinx was put up more than forty-five hundred years ago are always dismissed, evidence be damned. The Ministry of Antiquities is invested in their timeline. Anyone who contradicts the official history is considered a crank and a troublemaker."

"Everyone's been all over the Sphinx," Elizabeth said. "If there were any hidden chambers they would've been found a long time ago."

"That's just it," Selena said. "They did find them. There are also several underground tunnels in the area. Most of them have never been opened. The authorities don't allow exploration."

"Why not?" Lamont asked.

"For one thing, Egypt is Muslim. The Sphinx is an image forbidden by the Quran. The pyramids are considered an expression of human arrogance, an affront to Allah. Doing anything there stirs up trouble. Aside from that, the idea that someone other than Egyptians built the Sphinx is unacceptable. The last thing the authorities want to find are ancient records left by a different civilization."

"I'm surprised ISIS hasn't gone after the Sphinx by now," Nick said. "It's a perfect target. Think of the publicity if they blew it up."

"Assholes," Lamont said.

"Yeah. Assholes with guns and Semtex," Ronnie said.

Elizabeth rapped her pen on her desk. The hard sound came through the phone.

"Let's stay focused. Selena, are you positive your translation is accurate?"

"The only way to be sure is to find the archive."

"Under the Sphinx."

"Yes. We have to investigate it."

"It's been hidden for thousands of years."

"There's a sealed passage in the great pyramid. We can get to it through that."

"Good luck getting permission to open it up," Nick said.

"Who said anything about getting permission?"

"What sealed passage?" Elizabeth asked.

"The Egyptians found a hidden entrance in the great pyramid last year. They think it leads to a tunnel going to the Sphinx. We should get into the pyramid and open it. If there is a passage there, it will take us to the archive."

"If that's where it goes," Elizabeth said. "Let me be sure I understand you. You want to go into one of the biggest and most important historical attractions of the ancient world and break into a sealed entrance without getting caught. Then you want to follow a passage that might or might not be there to an archive that might not exist and discover what may be only a figment of someone's vivid imagination. Is that about it?"

"More or less."

"That is absolutely crazy."

"I wouldn't put it that way," Selena said. "I'd look at it as a challenge."

"A challenge?"

Nick interrupted. "It might not be too difficult, Director. Tourism is way off because of ISIS. If you can get us into the country without being arrested, we can bribe our way into the pyramid. The guards have been letting people in there for years who wanted to spend a night inside. We could be one more group of dumb foreigners. Selena's Arabic will help. A little C4 will get us into that passage."

"You're awfully quick to blow things up," Elizabeth said. "Now you want to damage a world monument."

"It's the only way to do it."

They waited while Elizabeth thought about it.

"There was an item in the morning brief two days ago. It looks like ISIS is planning a major attack in Egypt."

"How does that help?" Selena asked.

"For the moment the Egyptians are back to being our friends. I could offer to assist in preventing it."

"They may be acting like friends for now but I wouldn't count on it for much longer," Nick said. "Besides, they have their own counterterrorism unit."

"I know the general who runs internal security. I think I can convince him to let you enter the country. If he wants it done, it will happen."

Someone knocked on the cabin door. Nick opened it. It was John, the second mate.

"Take a look outside," he said.

Nick went over to the porthole. Not far away, the surface of the ocean churned and roiled. The air smelled of sulfur.

"Better come to the communication room," John said.

"Director, I have to go. Something's happening."

"Keep me posted," Elizabeth said.

They followed the mate to the communications room.

"What's up?" Nick said.

Sexton pointed at the ROV monitor. "Take a look."

The robot was outside the pyramid, about a quarter-mile from the ship. Yesterday there had been one or two vapor columns rising near the base of the massive structure. Now there were more than a dozen. It looked as though the seafloor near the pyramid was bulging.

"Is that what's making the disturbance on the surface?"

"You figured it out in one," Sexton said. "Something's getting ready to blow down there. Probably a volcano."

"A volcano?"

"Looks like it. Vicky, bring the rover home."

"What about the one we lost?" she asked.

"I don't want to lose this one too. If nothing happens down there we'll come back for it another time."

Vicky worked the joystick. The ROV backed away from the pyramid.

"What happens if it blows?" Selena asked.

"It depends. It's a long way down. It would take a really big eruption to sink us, but I'm not going to risk it. We're leaving."

Lamont pointed at the screen. "Something's happening."

Wide cracks appeared in the seabed, glowing with a malevolent, fiery red. The cracks spread outward from the pyramid.

"I think the pyramid's moving," Selena said.

"It can't move," Nick said. "How could it move?"

As they watched, the massive structure began to tilt. The seafloor around it split open. Then the pyramid began to slip away into the Atlantic abyss. It slid out of sight in a cloud of silt and steam. A glowing red column of molten lava fountained up from the shattered seabed.

The feed from the camera went dark.

Sexton ran to the bridge, yelling orders. Nick and the others followed him. By the time they got there the big diesels that drove *Sexton's Dream* had powered up and settled to a steady vibration.

"All ahead full. Flank speed."

"Flank speed, aye," the helmsman answered.

The ship began to move. The surface of the ocean foamed and curled. Suddenly a tall geyser of superheated water shot into the air. The column reached its peak and fell back., Scalding water and steaming rocks dropped onto the boat, a black rain from hell.

A glowing rock smashed through the skylight over the bridge and struck the second mate, knocking him to the deck. He screamed as his clothes caught fire. Two of the crew ran to help. Fires started on deck, where more rocks had landed.

Sexton yelled, "Get those fires out!"

A wave that looked as big as a house rushed toward them.

"Hang on!" Nick shouted

"Holy shit," Lamont said.

The wave struck the *Sexton's Dream*. The ship heeled over, sending everything that wasn't tied down flying through the air. Water cascaded over the decks and through the open door of the bridge. Slowly the ship righted itself.

Ahead lay the *Tolstoy*. The wave struck the bigger ship and swept across the decks. It continued on, subsiding as it moved away from the ships. Soon it was invisible. As it crossed the ocean it would build force until it became a tsunami.

"Whoa," Ronnie said.

The Russian ship appeared to have taken little damage. As the *Tolstoy* receded behind them. Selena saw Valentina come out onto the deck below the bridge.

The two sisters looked at each other as the distance between them increased.

CHAPTER 44

Valentina called General Vysotsky and told him what had happened.

"We sent an ROV down. There's nothing left. The pyramid and everything else is gone."

"*Der'mo.*"

"The Americans have sailed."

"We're tracking them," Vysotsky said. "They're heading back to Cairo. The pictures you sent of the writing in that pyramid are being translated as we speak."

"My sister has done that by now. Harker's people will act on whatever they discovered. The *Tolstoy* is still out of commission. I need to get back to the mainland."

"I agree. A helicopter will retrieve you and Major Rostov. It should arrive within the hour."

"Can't we leave her here?"

"Much as I would like to, it isn't an option. Orlov is watching. He's playing me against Volkov. He also has his eye on you, to see how you handle the situation. You're stuck with Rostov for now."

"What are my orders? "

"This mission has been a fiasco for Rostov. The only thing she has to show for the deaths of her men are those pictures. If they provide new information to lead to the archive, the two of you will pursue it. In that case her best chance to redeem herself with Volkov is to sabotage us. You will be there to stop her."

"I understand."

"You will arrive in Egypt before the Americans. Follow them. Do not allow yourself to be seen. If Rostov interferes, eliminate her. If you do, make sure it looks like an accident. You understand?"

"Yes."

"Yes, what?"

"Yes, sir."

"That's better. Keep me informed."

Valentina put her phone away as Rostov approached.

"I have just spoken with General Volkov," Rostov said. "It seems we must continue working together."

"A helicopter is coming for us."

"So he told me."

"We'll be waiting for the Americans when they arrive," Valentina said. "What they do next will determine our own actions."

"A sensible plan."

"I'm glad you agree. For now we will observe."

"And if they have found the archive?"

"Then they will go there and we will follow them," Valentina said.

"And then?"

"What do you think we should do, Rostov?"

"Once we're certain they are in the right place, we should intervene."

"Intervene?"

"We can't let them send anything back."

"How do you propose to stop them?"

"If necessary, we kill them."

"You'd like that, wouldn't you? Has it occurred to you that there will be retaliation if we kill them?"

"There's nothing the Americans can do. There may be a few incidents with our operatives outside the country. Of course that has more significance for your department than for mine. Aside from that, nobody's going to start a war because of a few dead spies."

Rostov smiled at her.

"I can see you don't like the idea. Is it because your sister is among them? I'm sure Moscow would be interested to see you put loyalty to an American spy above patriotism."

"Do not question my loyalty, Rostov. If I were you, I'd be more concerned about losing everyone under your command. It shows bad judgment. But that's nothing new for you."

"You think Vysotsky can protect you," Rostov said. "You could be right. But what if you aren't? You have much to learn, Antipov."

We'll see who has much to learn, Valentina thought.

In the distance she heard the *throp throp throp* of a helicopter approaching.

CHAPTER 45

General Basu Karimi's enormous gut was only the outward sign of his large appetites. Food was the least of his addictions. Karimi was fond of thin women, morphine and expensive liquor, though the last two were frowned upon by his religion. His face was broad, pocked with acne scars, his lips swollen and purplish from the digestive problems that arose from his gluttony. Thick black hair was slicked back on his moon-shaped head. His hands were almost dainty for such a coarse man, the nails manicured and covered with clear polish.

General Karimi was chief of the Egyptian secret police, the most feared and hated man in Egypt, a man whose name was used to frighten disobedient children. His uniforms were tailored to fit his huge girth and adorned with rows of medals. He looked like an Egyptian version of Hermann Goering. Like Goering, Karimi was a shrewd and dangerous man.

In the great political game playing out in the Middle East between America and Russia, Karimi was an important player. He'd grown rich accepting what he called "charitable donations" to secure his influence. Washington and Moscow both thought he was on their side and useful, if corrupt. The only side Karimi was on was his own.

When his aide told him Elizabeth Harker was on the phone, he felt a glow of satisfaction. His bank account was about to grow fatter. Whatever she wanted, it would not come cheaply. That she wanted something, he was sure. Why else would she call?

"Director Harker. It has been too long since I had the pleasure of hearing your voice."

In Virginia, Elizabeth put the Egyptian general on the speaker so Stephanie could listen. Karimi's voice oozed false charm. Stephanie pointed a finger at her mouth and made a gagging gesture. Elizabeth almost broke out laughing but stopped herself in time.

"General. Thank you for taking my call. I trust you are well?"

"My health is good, Allah be praised. Director, you have been very naughty. Your operatives created many problems for me in Marsá Matruh. It was very bad for business. I am unhappy."

"I am desolated by your unhappiness, General. Please accept my apologies. I'm sure some compensation can be arranged for your inconvenience. Perhaps a donation to one of your charities would help soothe your discomfort?"

"Your generosity is not unappreciated, Director."

"A contribution will be made in the regular way," Elizabeth said.

"Excellent," Karimi said.

"I'm glad to clear up any misunderstanding about what happened before. However, that's not why I'm calling. We have information ISIS is planning an attack near Cairo. I felt that because of your official role you should be aware it."

ISIS was a sore point for General Karimi. They were a spreading cancer, creating problems throughout the country. Karimi was under pressure to expose their followers and arrest them.

"Those lunatics are always planning trouble. We have handled them successfully in the past. How accurate is this information?"

"Of the highest accuracy. The attack will come soon. We believe it is aimed at your president. It's to our mutual advantage to prevent them from succeeding. I would like to assist you."

Now we're getting to it, Karimi thought.

"What kind of assistance?"

"I would like to send in my team. After the unfortunate events at the hotel, I need your cooperation for them to enter your country. They will not get in your way. Whatever they discover will immediately be made available to you."

"What do you think they can find out that my agents cannot?"

"ISIS has ties into the Western community in Egypt. My people have a much better chance of rooting out those connections than you do."

"I would say that depends on the situation." Karimi's voice was hard.

Elizabeth was well aware of Karimi's interrogation methods.

"We believe ISIS is ready to put their plan into action. There isn't much time for, uh, traditional techniques to be effective. My people are very good at what they do. You have nothing to lose and you will have the assistance of my government helping you without any appearance of dependence on the West. Needless to say, a large contribution to your favorite charity would be appropriate."

It was what Karimi needed to hear.

"I'm sure something can be arranged."

"In that case, I'll arrange the transfer of funds immediately. My team will arrive tomorrow. It's a pleasure to do business with you, General."

"I am always happy to help, Director."

After the call, Karimi leaned back in his chair and considered his options. He didn't believe for a minute that Harker wanted to assist him in thwarting a possible terrorist attack. She had some other goal in mind. The Americans were usually quite obvious in their manipulations but Harker was a different sort. Of course she was a woman, and all women were devious in their thinking.

Whatever she was after was certain to interest the Russians. Karimi had no reservations about playing one side against the other. He took out a small, black notebook and turned pages until he came to the entry he was looking for, a man who could be counted on to make a sizable donation in return for useful information.

He picked up his secured phone and called General Volkov in Moscow.

CHAPTER 46

There were no problems entering Egypt. They booked into a hotel on the edge of the Giza complex. The Great Pyramid of Khufu filled the view outside the windows of Nick and Selena's room. The lesser pyramids of Khafre and Menakaure were visible as well.

Lamont and Ronnie came in. Lamont went over to the window.

"That must've been pretty impressive when it was new," he said.

"Still is," Ronnie said.

Selena pointed at the peak. "You can still see some of the white limestone they used to cover it when it was new. The facing was stripped off and used for buildings in Cairo."

"Let's figure out what we're going to do," Nick said.

Selena opened up her laptop. "I talked with Stephanie on the way here. She sent me plans of the pyramid and an article about that sealed entrance. You see the long descending passage? What we're after is about halfway between ground level and the pit, on the left as you're going down. That's in the direction of the Sphinx."

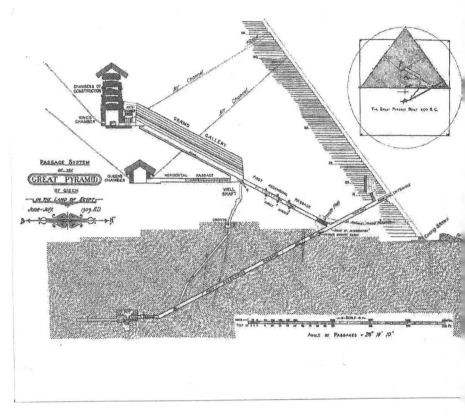

"I thought the Sphinx was in front of the Great Pyramid," Ronnie said.

"No. It's at the end of a buried causeway that leads from the pyramid of Khafre. That's the next one over."

"I've never seen the pyramids except in pictures," Lamont said.

"You'll get a good look at them this afternoon," Nick said. "We'll hire a guide and do an initial recon."

"We have time for lunch before that?" Lamont said.

CHAPTER 47

Karimi's aide came to the open door of his office.

"General, the Russian woman is here."

"Send her in."

Karimi belched and thought about his growing bank account. The call to General Volkov had been most productive.

The aide escorted the woman into Karimi's office and left, closing the door. His eyes wandered over her body. She was tall and thin, the kind of look that appealed to him. Her black hair was cropped short over cold, black eyes. He could see no jewelry. She was attractive in a harsh way, all angles and planes. He wondered if the rest of her was as hard as her face.

"General. Thank you for seeing me on such short notice. I am Major Katerina Rostov."

"General Volkov told me about you, Major. Please, sit down. I can give you ten minutes."

Katerina smiled at him.

"General Volkov speaks of you with admiration," Rostov said.

Bullshit, Karimi thought.

He smiled back at her. "That is most gratifying. I am a great admirer of the Russian security services."

"I will come directly to the point, General. Director Volkov says you are aware that American spies have entered your country. I've been instructed to seek your cooperation."

"Go on."

"These *svolochi* are in possession of information of vital importance to our country. With your permission, we will observe them and try to recover it."

"What information are we speaking of?"

"I don't know. I am told it is highly classified and critical to our national security."

Karimi heard the words roll off Katerina Rostov's tongue as if she were discussing the time of day.

Only a fool would believe that. He pretended to consider what she had said.

"I am willing to give permission on the condition that you do not interfere with them at this time. I, too, wish to observe. I want to know why they are here. Once I know that, I will arrest them and allow you to interrogate them."

"General..."

Karimi let a hard edge creep into his voice. "That is my decision."

"Of course." Rostov stood. "Your help is appreciated. We will observe only."

"If you find anything, inform me immediately. For our mutual benefit."

A threat, Katerina thought. *What a pig, look at him. Why are men like him always the same? He has to make sure I know who's boss.*

"As you wish."

"My aide will show you out."

He pressed a button on his desk. The door opened and the aide waited.

Karimi hoisted his bulk out of his chair, a small concession.

"Thank you for coming to me. I am always ready to assist the Federation."

The woman nodded and followed the aide out. Karimi watched them go. Everyone wanted to take advantage of the turmoil of modern Egypt. Spies and plots had been part of Egypt's history since the days of the pharaohs. These foreign newcomers would soon learn they were amateurs when it came to the art of conspiracy.

CHAPTER 48

Nick hired a guide who introduced himself as Gamal. The original way into the great pyramid was blocked by stone. The current entrance dated from the ninth century CE. It was called the robbers' tunnel and opened onto the descending passage. They followed Gamal downward until they came to a junction with another tunnel that turned up at an angle.

Gamal's English was good.

"This is the ascending passage," he said. "It leads to the Grand Gallery, the Queen's chamber and the King's Chamber."

"What happens if we continue down?" Selena asked with an innocent expression.

"That leads to the subterranean chamber."

"I'd like to see that," she said.

"There is little to see down there," Gamal said. "Perhaps there will be time later. Come, this way."

They climbed until they came to a level passage that led to the Queen's Chamber. All the while the guide kept up his memorized commentary. The Queen's Chamber was large, empty. A tall, stepped niche that looked like an open chimney rose to a high peaked ceiling made of large slabs of stone. Modern electric lighting lit the limestone walls.

Gamal stood in front of the niche. "A statue of the dead Pharaoh once stood here," he said. His voice was mechanical. "Traces of offerings were found. You can see where at one time there was an altar in front of the niche. The entrance to the chamber was hidden."

They left the Queen's Chamber and went back to the ascending passage. They followed it upward through the Grand Gallery to the King's Chamber. Ronnie and Lamont lagged behind as the guide droned on.

"Does this guy ever shut up?" Lamont asked.

"Nope."

"Maybe we could bribe him."

"Think of it as an education," Ronnie said.

They entered the King's Chamber. Gamal pointed out various features. Ventilation shafts let cool air into the room and kept the temperature at a steady 68°. The only thing in the room was a large, broken sarcophagus of plain granite thought to have held the pharaoh's remains. Surveillance cameras were mounted near the ceiling.

"There's something sad about this," Selena said, "all these empty rooms and passageways."

"We must go back now," Gamal said.

"Not before we see the subterranean chamber," Selena said.

"This will require a small increase in my fee."

"That's not a problem," Nick said. "We appreciate your excellent services."

Gamal preened at the complement.

"Come then."

They descended to the junction with the ascending passage and continued past it toward the subterranean chamber. The passage was lit with a string of electric lights. Nick watched for any sign of the hidden entrance. By the time they reached the bottom, he'd seen nothing to tell him where it was.

The subterranean chamber was no more than a rough grotto hewn out of bedrock under the pyramid. A pit at the back was sealed off with a metal fence.

"Man, this is creepy," Lamont said. "I can feel all that stone over us. If that roof gave way we'd be crushed flat."

"It's not going to fall on you," Nick said.

"It looks like it was never finished," Ronnie said. "Everything else is. I wonder why?"

"It's one of the mysteries of the pyramid," Selena said. "There are a lot of those. People argue about what things were for. Some people think the pyramid was really an observatory but that's not popular with the Egyptologists. Anything that goes against the idea it was a tomb is ignored."

"There are many mysteries about the pyramid," the guide said. He looked at his watch, a large, cheap model with a plastic strap. "It is getting late. We must go before the entrance closes."

They followed him out into the late afternoon sunlight. The heat struck them as they emerged from the cool interior of the pyramid.

Nick took Selena aside. "Talk to him. Make up a story about why we want to be inside at night. Offer him whatever he wants."

Selena went over to Gamal and began speaking with him in Arabic. He looked shocked that she could speak his language. At first he shook his head, no. Nick saw Selena press money into Gamal's hand. After a few more minutes Selena came back. The guide walked away.

"He will meet us at ten this evening. He says the guard likes to have coffee in his shack about that time. Gamal will open the gate for us. After that, we're on our own and the gate will be locked. We'll be stuck inside until the complex opens in the morning. He warned me that strange things have happened to people who stayed in the pyramid overnight."

"I could see he didn't want to do it," Nick said. "What did you tell him to make him change his mind?"

"I told him we'd made a bet before we left home that we could spend a night in the pyramid. He understood that. If I'd said anything else, it wouldn't have worked. Also a hundred dollars American helped."

"Did you see any sign of that passage on the way down?"

"Maybe. I saw some discoloration on the wall. There wasn't time to stop and examine it."

"There'll be plenty of time tonight," Nick said.

CHAPTER 49

The pyramid loomed against the stars, an otherworldly, brooding presence in the night. They passed the guardhouse without incident. Gamal took them to an iron gate blocking the entrance at night. A large padlock held it shut. The guide produced a key from under his robe and opened it.

"Hurry," he said. "The guard will return soon."

They filed through. Lamont was last in line. He had a small pack with the C4 and detonators they'd need to break through the sealed entrance, assuming they could find it.

Gamal closed the gate behind them and snapped the lock shut with a harsh, metallic sound. He hurried away without looking back.

They entered the pyramid and turned on their flashlights, Nick in the lead. The brilliant lights danced over the walls of the ancient passage, casting harsh shadows. Ahead, the way descended into darkness.

"Looks different at night without the lights," Ronnie said.

"I thought it was creepy during the day," Lamont said. "This is worse."

They came to the junction with the ascending passage and continued downward.

"What we're looking for could be anywhere along here," Nick said.

"The discoloration I saw is a little further on," Selena said, "on the left-hand side."

They were about halfway between the junction and the subterranean chamber and well below ground level when Selena stopped them.

"Here."

She shone her light on the wall.

"See how the stone here is a little different from the rest of the wall? It's subtle. You'd never notice if you weren't looking for it."

"There's not much of a difference," Nick said.

"If there's a passage behind this, it was sealed a long time ago," Selena said. "It might have been done when the pyramid was built. The work is of the same quality."

"Why make a passage and then close it right away?" Ronnie asked.

"Who knows? Maybe there isn't a passage. It could be a chamber of some kind. Or nothing at all and this is only a different kind of stone."

"Let's find out," Lamont said.

He opened his pack, took out a lump of C4 and broke off a piece.

"What do you think?" he asked Ronnie. "At the corners? Or one in the middle? Or all along the side?"

"The middle sounds about right. That should work if there's an opening behind it and it's not too thick."

"Don't overdo it," Nick said. "If the roof comes down it will piss off a lot of people."

"You really gotta do something about that optimistic streak," Lamont said.

He kneaded the explosive into a lump and placed it against the stone, set a remote detonator and turned it on.

"All set."

They retreated back up the passage.

"This is far enough," Lamont said. "Fire in the hole."

They crouched down and covered their ears.

The explosion sent a shockwave of compressed air up the shaft, buffeting them with bits of stone and a cloud of white dust. The dust hung in the air like fog, drifting in the beams of their lights.

Ronnie sneezed. Selena began coughing. After a minute, the dust began to settle.

"Think they heard that outside?" Ronnie asked.

"Hard to say." Nick gestured up the passage. "We're pretty far underground. All that stone up there absorbs a lot of sound. Even if someone heard it, they wouldn't know what it was or where it came from."

He stood. "Time to see what we've got."

The floor was littered with pieces of broken limestone. They picked their way through the debris to a large hole in the wall. Beyond was tunnel high enough to walk in, leading away into the dark.

CHAPTER 50

Valentina and Major Rostov had watched the Americans enter the pyramid in the afternoon. Now they'd followed them into the complex at night. They watched the guide open the gate and let them through, lock the gate and walk away.

"I don't think they're sightseeing," Rostov said.

"I wonder what they're after?" Valentina said.

"Does it matter? We follow them."

They crept past the guard shack, keeping to the shadows. Arabic music and the sweet smell of Turkish tobacco mixed with hashish drifted out of the shack into the night air. They came to the iron gate. Valentina took out a set of picks and had the padlock open in less than a minute. They eased through the gate and closed it, leaving the lock in place. It looked as though the entrance was still sealed. They entered the pyramid.

The only way to go was down. They had just started when the muffled sound of the explosion pummeled their ears. Seconds later, a billowing cloud of dust swept past them. Valentina began coughing.

"Quiet," Rostov hissed.

"Someone might've heard that." Valentina wiped her eyes with the back of her hand.

"If someone follows us in, they will regret it," Rostov said. "Their security is laughable. The only one out there is the guard and he was listening to music. It's unlikely he heard or saw anything."

They came to the debris left by the blast and the opening in the wall. Rostov shone her light into the tunnel.

"Now we know why they came here," Rostov said, "to find and open this."

"This must lead to the archive."

"They've gone in." Rostov stepped through the opening and drew her pistol. "Coming?"

Some distance ahead, Nick led the others in single file along the ancient tunnel. The air was stale and hot, heavy with the passage of time. They came to a place where the tunnel widened and split in three directions. Black shapes scuttled away from their lights, making clicking sounds.

"What was that?" Selena said.

"Scorpions," Nick said. "Big ones."

"How do we always end up in places like this?"

"I hate scorpions," Lamont said. "I saw enough of them in Iraq. Always crawling into your boots at night."

"Now what?" Ronnie said. "Which one do we take?"

"They all look the same," Lamont said.

Nick shone his light down the passage on the right. "This one is blocked. We're not going that way."

"What do we do, flip a coin?" Lamont aimed his light at the middle tunnel.

Selena moved her light over the openings. There was nothing to indicate which one to take or where it might lead. She shone her light on the third tunnel.

"The Sphinx is Southwest of the Great Pyramid. We've been going south. The center passage probably keeps going in the same direction. We should take the left-hand one."

"That makes sense," Nick said.

They started down the left-hand tunnel. Lamont kept glancing around, looking for scorpions. After a few minutes they came to another junction. This time it was a T.

"Right or left?" Nick said.

"Left." Selena pointed. "The Sphinx has to be to the left."

"Good a guess as any."

They had gone about a hundred yards when the tunnel opened into a circular room with four different passages leading away from it.

"Man, this place is like a maze," Lamont said. "Be easy to get lost in here."

Something was scratched on one of the walls. Selena walked over to it.

"We're in the right place. This is the Atlantis language."

"What does it say?" Ronnie asked.

"'Amon was here.'"

"You're kidding."

"That's what it says."

"Great," Nick said. "Ten thousand-year-old graffiti. Now what?"

Lamont took out a candy bar and began eating it. Ronnie looked at him and shook his head.

Selena said, "We have to be close to the Sphinx."

She knelt down in the dust on the floor and began drawing a map with her finger. The others watched as she drew a square.

"This is the Great Pyramid. We started from the south side."

She drew a smaller square, this one below and to the left of the first.

"This is the pyramid of Khafre."

She traced a long line angling down and away from Khafre's pyramid. At the end of it she drew a little square. Next to that she drew a larger rectangle.

"The line is the buried causeway. At the end of that are the ruins of a temple. The rectangle next to that is the Sphinx."

"Where are we in that drawing?" Ronnie asked.

Selena drew a straight line away from the great pyramid. About halfway to the causeway she drew the first junction they had come to, with three passages. She drew another line angling down and marked the T junction, stopping before she reached the causeway. She drew a line from that and stopped. She made four dots in the dust to indicate openings.

"I think we're here, at these dots."

They looked at what she had drawn.

"If you're right, we should take this one." Nick pointed at the third dot she'd made. "That should lead to the Sphinx."

"Now would be a good time to talk about traps," Selena said.

"You mean like we saw in Tibet?"

"Not again," Ronnie said.

"What traps?" Lamont asked.

"False floors, rolling boulders, spikes that pop out. Spears that shoot out of the walls. Things that drop on you."

Lamont sighed. "You're saying the roof could fall in on us? Thanks a lot."

"There might not be any traps," Selena said, "but I think we ought to be careful. If we're looking, we should be able to avoid them. Just go slow."

"I'll go first," Nick said.

Nick played his light over the entrance of the third opening. It was wide enough for two to walk abreast.

"This one is different. Look at the way it's made. It's square. The walls and floor are finished, smooth."

"We must be getting close to something," Selena said.

They'd gone no more than a hundred paces into the passage when it ended in a granite slab blocking the way. Chiseled into the center of the stone was an elaborate circular carving. Ten sea creatures were set at regular intervals around the circumference, like the numbers on a clock. Each creature was carved on a raised, round stone. Each stone bore a single character in the language of Atlantis. There were dolphins, a shark, an octopus and several kinds of fish, all carved with lifelike precision. Underneath the central design were two more rows of characters in the Atlantean language.

"That looks pretty solid," Ronnie said.

Nick ran his hand over the writing. "Selena, what does this say?"

"Give me a minute."

She stood in front of the wall, concentrating on the strange letters while the others held their lights on the carving.

"It's a dedication to the ruler and a warning not to go any farther. This is a door."

"A door? How are we supposed to open it?"

"The raised characters around the outside of the circle are a combination. You have to press them in the right sequence."

"We'll never figure that out," Nick said. "We'll have to blow it."

"I don't think we can," Ronnie said. "That looks pretty solid. The amount of C4 we'd have to use could seal the tunnel."

"You have a better idea?"

"Figure out the combination."

Lamont pointed his light at the finished ceiling of the passage.

"I think there's a trap up there." They all looked up. "See those lines in the stone?"

The faint outline of a thick rectangle as wide as the door was just visible.

"He's right," Selena said. "That would account for the warning. It's probably rigged to drop down if someone punches in the wrong combination. It would block anyone who wasn't supposed to be here from getting through."

"Yeah, and crush you like a bug at the same time," Lamont said.

"Even if we could blow through the door, that stone would drop," Selena said. "It must be three feet thick. We wouldn't get through that."

"This has to be the right place," Nick said. "Is there anything in that writing to help us get through?"

"The opposite. It says the gods will curse and destroy anyone who dares to enter."

"Guess these folks weren't very friendly," Lamont said.

Selena studied the carving. "Let me think."

Lamont made sure he was standing away from where the stone might fall. He took out another candy bar and began unwrapping it.

"Don't you ever get tired of eating that junk?" Ronnie asked.

"Gives me energy. You want one?" Lamont took a large bite.

"Now I know why you're getting fat."

"Fat?" Lamont looked down at his stomach. "I'm not the one pushing out over his belt."

"That's muscle, not fat," Ronnie said.

"Will you two be quiet?" Selena said. "I'm trying to think."

She looked at the ten characters circling the design. They weren't numbers or the names of the creatures. Each character was one word. The combination was a phrase. She tried reading them in sequence but it made no sense.

Two of the symbols were unfamiliar. She'd seen the rest before, some the first time she'd seen the unknown writing, in the photograph sent by the Russian. She sorted the characters in her mind. They fell into place.

"I think I've got it."

She stepped forward and pushed against a stone with a fish on it. It sank into the slab. There was a grinding noise. Something moved behind the stone face of the door.

"Selena, wait," Nick said. "You're under the trap."

"We don't have anything long enough to push these in."

"What if you're wrong?"

"If I don't do this we're not getting in there."

She reached up and pushed a second stone, this one carved with a dolphin. Again there was a sound of a mechanism moving inside the door. A trickle of fine dust dropped from the ceiling above.

"Wait a minute," Nick said.

Selena pressed a third time. More dust fell from the ceiling.

"Oh, shit," Ronnie said

"One to go."

Selena pressed the last stone and did a quick back flip away from the door, landing on her feet.

A loud rumbling and clanking came from within the walls. The floor shook under their feet. The stone door swung open.

Dim light flickered beyond.

"Open, sesame," Selena said.

CHAPTER 51

"Damn it, Selena, you scared the hell out of me," Nick said. "What if you'd been wrong?"

"But I wasn't, was I? Besides, I would've gotten out of the way before that rock fell on me."

"Maybe. Maybe not. What was the combination?"

"Homeland. It's not one word, it's a four character phrase. The characters were on the design. I just had to put them in sequence. Nothing else made sense."

"Pretty ballsy," Lamont said.

"I'll take that as a compliment," Selena said.

"Wow," Ronnie said, "look at that."

The door opened onto a room two hundred feet long and half as wide. The walls were made of fitted stone, the work of a master mason. A soft, bluish green light came from flickering strips on the walls. Sections of the strips were dark but there was enough light to see hundreds of wooden chests arranged in neat rows. In the center of the room was a table. On top of the table was a smaller chest.

Nick took a step and felt something crunch under his boot. He looked down.

"Watch for scorpions. These black ones are really nasty."

"Why are there always bugs?" Ronnie muttered.

"Technically, a scorpion isn't a bug," Lamont said.

"What are you, mister nature man? It crawls, it's got too many legs and it bites. It's a bug."

"Scorpions sting, they don't bite."

"Whatever."

"I don't believe this," Selena said.

"It's real enough," Nick said.

She walked over to the nearest chest and tried the lid. It was fastened with leather hinges. They fell apart as she opened the chest. She set the lid on the floor.

"What's inside?"

"Scrolls. It's full of scrolls."

"You think all these chests are like that?" Ronnie asked.

"Probably."

She picked up a scroll. It crumbled into fragments.

"I hope that wasn't what we're looking for," Nick said.

"It will take years to sort through this. If these chests are full of scrolls, each one will have to be treated before it can be opened up and read. It may not even be possible."

"That's not our concern. We've done what we came here to do, find this archive. We'll leave the rest to the politicians."

"How do these lights work?" Lamont said.

Nick looked at the flickering strips. "Probably some kind of phosphorus. Or a chemical compound. Pretty impressive that it still works after all this time."

"The Egyptians are going to go nuts when they learn about this," Selena said. "This room was here long before the pharaohs showed up on the scene. It's proof their historical timeline is wrong."

"When do you think all this stuff was stashed in here?" Ronnie asked.

"If the people who left all this are the same ones who carved out the Sphinx, ten or twelve thousand years."

"What do we do now?" Lamont asked.

Selena threaded her way through the chests until she reached the chest in the middle. She lifted the lid and looked down.

"Oh, my."

Selena reached into the chest and took out a smooth object a little larger than a football, rounded at the ends. It was translucent, scarred with black pits and long scorch marks as if it had been through an intense fire. It felt warm and heavy in her hands. She held it up for them to see. It began to glow with soft, blue light.

"That's really something," Lamont said.

"The Stone of the Gods," Nick said.

"It has to be." Selena turned it in her hands. "It almost feels alive. It's getting warmer as I hold it."

"Better put it back in the box," Nick said.

Selena placed the stone in the chest and closed the lid. She picked the chest up and walked back to the others.

"I think it must be a kind of meteor," she said. "I wonder how they made it work?"

"Someone will figure it out. We're done here," Nick said. "We'll go back to the surface and call Harker."

"*I don't think so.*"

The voice came from the doorway behind them. They turned to see Rostov pointing a pistol at them. Valentina stood beside her, a pistol in her hand.

"Valentina!"

"Hello, sister. We really have to stop meeting like this."

"How... What are you doing here?"

Valentina waved her pistol at the room. "The same thing as you. Looking for this room and what's in that chest you're holding."

Rostov pointed her pistol at Selena.

"Put the chest down."

Selena set it on the floor.

Rostov swiveled her pistol to Nick.

"Tell them to take their weapons out and lay them on the floor. Any attempt to fight, I kill you. I warn you, this pistol has a sensitive trigger. Be careful. My finger is nervous."

Nick looked at the wrong end of Rostov's Makarov. The barrel was steady. He looked at her eyes. She wasn't bluffing.

"Do as she says."

He drew his pistol with two fingers, bent down and laid it on the floor. The others followed suit.

"Good dogs," Rostov said. "Now kick them away."

The guns scraped across the floor.

"Get over there, against the wall."

"Let's talk about this," Nick said.

"Against the wall. I won't ask again."

They lined up against the wall.

"What are we going to do with them?" Valentina asked.

"What do you think?"

"You can't kill them."

"Why not?"

"These people aren't low level agents. The consequences would be bad. The Americans will retaliate."

"You think we should let them go?"

"Look at this room," Valentina said. "There isn't any way to keep this secret. What do you think will happen when they come in here and find four dead bodies?"

"They won't find four," Rostov said. "They'll find five."

She turned and shot Valentina. Selena's sister staggered sideways and fell. Her pistol clattered on the floor toward Selena. Ronnie reached for the gun in his ankle holster. Nick and Lamont dove for their weapons. Selena ducked down and grabbed Valentina's gun as Rostov fired at her. The bullet missed and ricocheted off the wall into one of the flickering light strips. A viscous waterfall of green gushed out and splashed onto the wooden chests below.

The ancient wood ignited in a burst of flame. The room began to fill with black, oily smoke.

Nick picked his gun off the floor, raised up and fired at Rostov. He missed. She backed away to the entrance and through the doorway, firing as she went. Smoke swirled past her, sucked into the passage behind. Nick fired again. Rostov went down. As she fell, her pistol went off.

The bullet struck the ceiling above and triggered the trap. A slab of granite dropped from the ceiling and crushed her, cutting off her scream. It sounded as though someone had stepped on a very large bug. Blood oozed out from under the stone.

"Jesus," Lamont said.

Selena bent over Valentina. Rostov's bullet had entered her side.

"I didn't know she was going to do that," Valentina said. Her voice was strained.

"She's dead." Selena said.

"Good."

The fire was spreading.

Nick came over. "Selena, we have to get out of here."

"Valentina, can you stand?"

"Maybe. Help me."

"Nick, help me lift her."

Valentina gasped with pain as they pulled her to her feet.

Smoke hung in a dark cloud below the ceiling of the room. The wooden chests popped and crackled as the flames reached them and the ancient parchments inside ignited.

Ronnie said. "How do we get out of here? The entrance is blocked."

"Blow it."

"Ain't happening," Lamont said.

A wall of flame stood between them and the entrance. They retreated to the other end of the long room, coughing in the thick smoke. Nick and Selena supported Valentina between them. Nick looked at the advancing flames. It wouldn't be long before the fire got to them or they ran out of air.

"Look," Ronnie said. "Scorpions."

A stream of panicked scorpions scurried toward the back wall where they stood. They were coming out of the chests, dozens of them. The sound of their claws clicking and clattering as they scrabbled across the stone floor made a bizarre counterpoint to the crackling of the flames.

Lamont took out his pistol.

"Forget about it, Lamont. They're going somewhere."

More scorpions appeared, a steady stream. The head of the stream reached the wall and disappeared, the others following behind.

"Where are they going?" Selena asked.

"There must be another passage behind that wall," Nick said, "a way out."

The fire worked its way toward them down the rows of chests. The crackling of the flames had turned into a steady roar. The layer of smoke on the ceiling had dropped to a foot above their heads.

The wall where the scorpions had vanished was covered with tiled squares, each one marked with a character in the language of Atlantis. Selena felt the heat of the fire on her back as she looked at the wall. She tried to understand what she was seeing.

Was it a combination of things, like the entrance? Was it a single tile? There was no time to study it. Snapping noises came from the burning chests behind her as the flames came closer.

If I'm in the room, she thought, *I don't need a combination to get out of it.*

"Start pressing tiles," she called over the roar of the fire. "One of them has to be the key."

They began to press against the tiles. It was getting hard to see and hard to breathe. Valentina leaned against the wall.

Ronnie felt a tile sink into the wall under his hand. A hidden door opened at the corner where the scorpions had gone, revealing another tunnel.

Coughing and bent low to keep under the smoke, they hurried to the doorway and into the passage beyond. Nick took the lead. Ronnie and Lamont had Valentina between them. Selena brought up the rear.

The scorpions were nowhere to be seen. Smoke poured into the tunnel.

"Keep moving," Nick said.

"I hope this doesn't lead to a dead end," Lamont said.

After a few minutes they came to an iron grill blocking the way.

Nick gripped it. "This isn't old. It must've been put up to keep people out of this tunnel."

Lamont looked at the gate. "It won't take much to blow it."

He took C4 from his pack and began working. The smoke was thicker.

"Move back."

He detonated the charge. The grill fell away, clanging against the floor. They stepped over it and found themselves in a lightless chamber with a rounded wall.

Selena played her flashlight over the interior of the chamber, then along the wall.

"There's an opening over there. It's been sealed with cement."

"Seems to be our day for breaking things open," Nick said.

"That cement looks old," Lamont said.

"Blow it before the smoke gets any worse."

Lamont placed the last bit of C4 against the walled up opening. They retreated to the far corner and detonated the charge. Fresh air blew into the chamber.

They climbed through the opening and out into the Egyptian night. Nick looked up at the stars and took a deep breath of cool air.

"Look where we are," Selena said.

They stood next to the Sphinx. The opening was in the right hind leg of the statue.

"You were right all along," Nick said.

"Everything's gone," she said. "All those records. Safe for ten thousand years and now they're gone. The history of a civilization."

"And the Stone of the Gods. Don't forget that. Nobody will ever know what it was or how they used it."

The smoke had found its way to the opening. A lazy column drifted out of the Sphinx.

"Take a look at the pyramid," Ronnie said.

A column of black smoke rose from the pyramid entrance.

Lamont sneezed. "Might be time to get out of here."

Valentina slumped unconscious between Ronnie and Selena.

"We need to get help for her," Selena said.

They almost made it to the parking lot before the police surrounded them.

CHAPTER 52

General Basu Karimi had put the prisoners in isolation. None of the police who'd arrested them would talk. Not if they knew what was good for them.

The Ministry of Antiquities screamed for the heads of the vandals who had defiled the ancient symbols of Egypt. They didn't know Karimi had them in custody. They weren't going to know, unless he decided to tell them.

Karimi had moved his prisoners to a private facility outside of Cairo that he used for special interrogations. The place had a dark reputation. No one would bother him there. He'd arranged medical care for Valentina. Now he waited for his aide to bring the American leader to him.

Nick entered the room.

"Leave us," Karimi said to his aide.

"General. Are you sure? This man is a threat."

"Are you deaf? Leave us." His voice was full of menace.

The man left the room and closed the door behind him.

"Sit down."

Karimi indicated a hard chair in front of his desk. Nick sat down.

"I know who you are. You are part of a covert team sent here by your director, Harker. It was I who allowed you to enter my country."

"You have an advantage over me."

"Ah, please excuse my rudeness. I am General Basu Karimi."

"The chief of the Mukhabharat?"

"I am pleased that you know of me. After a few formalities, you and your companions will be returned to America."

"What formalities?" Nick asked.

Karimi ignored the question. "What were you doing in the pyramid?"

"Would you believe me if I said we were sightseeing?"

"Please do not make the mistake of annoying me, Mister Carter. I know that you were looking for something. I know the Russians were looking for the same thing. By the way, where is Major Rostov?"

"She made a mistake. Right now she's pressed flatter than a postage stamp under tons of granite."

"That is unfortunate. Tell me about the fire."

There was no point in lying.

"We found a sealed tunnel in the descending passage of the pyramid. It led to a hidden room filled with wooden chests. The room was lit with strips of some phosphorescent material set on the walls. That's what caused the fire."

"How?"

"Rostov followed us in and was going to kill us. She shot Valentina and took a shot at Selena. The bullet hit one of the strips. Whatever was inside spilled out on the chests and everything began to burn."

"Why would Rostov shoot her associate?"

"I assume she had a grudge. Rostov was FSB. Valentina is SVR."

This was new information for Karimi. He would use it to leverage the Russians.

"What was in the chests? Gold? Artifacts?"

"No gold, General. We only opened one before Rostov showed up. It was full of parchment scrolls. As far as I know, they all were. Records. The room was an archive of Atlantis."

Nick saw no point in telling Karimi about the Stone of the Gods. What good would it do?

"Do not try to deceive me, Carter."

"I'm telling you the truth, General. Since you know who we are, you can ask Director Harker if you don't believe me."

"I will. You had better hope she verifies your story."

"Everything was destroyed," Nick said. "There's no reason to try and hide it. When your people get into that room they'll find plenty of evidence to back me up."

"The room no longer exists. It is filled with many tons of stone. The heat from the fire brought down the roof."

"Then you'll have to take my word for it."

"Why were you seeking this...archive?"

"We were looking for information about an unknown energy used by the Atlanteans to build their civilization. We thought those records would tell us what we needed to know, if we could find them. The same energy was probably used to move the stones in your pyramids and lift them into place."

Karimi gave him an incredulous look. "You expect me to believe that?"

"General, I don't expect anything. You asked me what we were doing there. I told you. I know you're not a man to be trifled with."

Karimi had considered torturing the Americans to get at the truth but had decided it would be more profitable to return them unharmed and claim a reasonable reward. Carter's story confirmed his decision. No one would make up a story like that and tell it to the man who could turn his life into agony.

"You said everything was destroyed."

"Yes. Wood doesn't get any drier than those chests. The fire went through them like they were soaked in gasoline."

Karimi pressed a button on his desk. The door opened. The aide waited for instructions.

"Take him back to the others."

Nick got up and walked out the door, the aide a step behind.

Karimi thought for a moment. First he would call Harker and see what she said about Carter's story. Then he would offer to return her operatives to America without unpleasant interference from the authorities, for a small consideration. That left the Russian.

Karimi had dealt with SVR in the past. He knew the director, Vysotsky, a reasonable man who understood how things worked in Egypt. Vysotsky would pay well for the return of his operative and the avoidance of bad publicity for the Federation.

That left the question of who would take the blame for defiling the pyramid and the Sphinx. The answer was simple. Karimi would blame everything on ISIS. It would be easy enough to round up suspects.

Visions of his ever-increasing bank account danced in his mind's eye. Karimi took out his satellite phone and called Director Harker.

CHAPTER 53

Women and men were kept in separate sections of Karimi's special interrogation center, but gender brought no benefits in accommodations. The walls were of cinderblock, the cell doors of iron bars. Prisoners slept on a dirt floor. Interrogations took place in a separate room, away from the cells. The cries of anyone unfortunate enough to be taken there could be heard throughout the building.

Huge cockroaches clustered around the stinking bucket that served as a toilet in Selena's cell. They showed no fear of her at all. She'd decided to relieve herself on the floor before she would use that bucket.

Valentina's cell was two down from hers. As far as Selena could tell, the rest of the cells in the short hallway were empty. When they'd first arrived there had been a woman in the next cell over, but she'd been taken away. Later, Selena had heard screaming. The woman hadn't returned.

Selena didn't want to think about what might have happened to her.

"Sister, can you hear me?" Valentina's voice was quiet.

"I hear you. Are you all right?"

"Yes. And you?"

"Yes. You tried to throw me your gun, didn't you? When we were in that room?"

"I knew I couldn't shoot Rostov before I went down," Valentina said. "That bitch got what she deserved."

"Why did she shoot you?"

Valentina gave a weak laugh. It turned into a prolonged fit of coughing. "She was like one of those scorpions. It was her nature. Her boss probably put her up to it."

"Volkov?"

"He is ambitious and jealous of my organization's success. He would like to bring back the KGB. I am sure General Vysotsky and myself would be at the top of his list for the courtyard at the Lubyanka and a bullet in the back of the head."

"I thought all that was over," Selena said.

"If you thought that you are naïve."

Selena was quiet. She thought about her father and his illegitimate daughter. Her sister.

"What are you thinking?" Valentina asked.

"I was thinking about our father."

"Your father, maybe. Not mine. Mine was a biological accident."

"If you like."

"You had a father. I had instructors."

"You had your mother. What was she like?"

"She was KGB. What do you think she was like?"

Oh, Valentina, you are so angry.

"It's strange," Selena said, "you and I."

"I know. I wish we were not enemies."

"We don't have to be. You could come to America."

Valentina started to laugh. It changed to coughing. "Why don't you come to Russia? I think that would be better."

"I'm serious. There's a place for you there."

"You really are naïve, aren't you, sister?"

Selena changed the subject. "What do you think they'll do with us?"

"We work for clever people, you and I. I think we will be going home soon."

"How did you know where the ruins were?"

"You mean in the ocean?"

"Yes."

"It was on the computer in your hotel room."

"You took it?"

11111111111111

11111

"You should be grateful it was me who found it and not Rostov. You and your friends are not very good at knowing when you are being watched."

The thought was chilling. Selena put it away for another time.

"Maybe you're better at concealment than you think."

"I'll take that as a compliment," Valentina said.

The outer door of their cellblock scraped open. Two guards came in. They stopped in front of Selena's cell. One of them took out a key and unlocked it.

"Come."

"What about her?"

"Never mind about her. Come."

As they escorted her out of the building, Selena heard Valentina call after her.

"Don't worry, sister. We'll see each other again."

I hope so, Selena thought.

CHAPTER 54

Karimi had released Valentina and sent her back to Moscow. General Alexei Vysotsky was reading her report for the third time, with satisfaction.

It was everything he needed to discredit Volkov with President Orlov. Rostov had been following Volkov's orders. If she hadn't interfered, the mysterious stone that controlled the ancient force would now be in the Kremlin's hands.

Orlov had become obsessed with thoughts of finding the archive of Atlantis. He'd demanded daily updates while the mission was unfolding. Now no one would ever know what had been in those records, or what might have been accomplished if the Atlantis stone had been brought back to Russia. The Americans had failed to get what they wanted, but that was of small comfort to the Russian president.

Orlov was angry.

Alexei was certain Volkov's story of events would be different from Valentina's. He was meeting with the president and Volkov in an hour at Orlov's office in the Kremlin. Alexei planned to bring Valentina with him and have her wait outside. It was obvious Orlov was attracted to her. He would want to hear her story in person. When he did, it would be Volkov's word against Valentina's. Alexei thought he knew who would be believed.

He was looking forward to the meeting.

His intercom sounded. "Major Antipov is here."

"Send her in."

When she entered the room Alexei saw she was in pain from her wound. Her face was pale and drawn. There were deep bags under her eyes.

Even better, Alexei thought. *Orlov will feel sorry for his little dove.*

"Valentina. Sit down. We have work to do today."

Alexei reached into his desk drawer and took out the vodka and two small glasses. He poured the liquor and handed her a glass.

"Drink this. It will help with the pain."

"*Na'zdrovnya*." They lifted glasses. She downed the shot. "What work?"

Alexei set his empty glass down on the desk.

"I am meeting with Orlov and Volkov in less than an hour. I'm taking you with me. You'll wait outside until I summon you."

"Should I be flattered? Why do you need me there?"

"You really must learn to curb your insolence, Valentina. Others may not be so tolerant of your petty rebellions."

Valentina bit back a sharp reply. "Yes, General."

"President Orlov will want to hear what happened from you."

"Doesn't he have my report?"

"Are you really so obtuse? Orlov wants to bed you. I want his desire to fuel his anger at Volkov."

"I suppose you would like me to seduce him."

"That would be an excellent result. Today would be a good day to begin. Nothing obvious, but I want you to plant the seed of an affair."

"And if I don't want to have sex with him?"

"Has that mattered in the past? It's an assignment, for the good of the nation."

Valentina wanted to point out that it was for the good of Vysotsky, not the nation. She kept her thoughts to herself. If she were honest, there was a certain attraction to seducing one of the most powerful men in the world. Getting him into bed would be easy. The challenge was whether or not she would be able to control him.

"You understand?" Alexei said.

"Yes."

"I want you to paint Rostov in the worst possible light. I want you to make sure Orlov knows she was acting under Volkov's direct orders when she decided to kill the Americans."

"Was she?" Valentina asked.

"It doesn't matter. What matters is the perception."

"Rostov was a bitch. I won't have any trouble describing her."

Alexei looked at his watch. "A car should be waiting downstairs for us. One more thing."

"Yes?"

"Limp a little when you come into the room. You are the wounded soldier, betrayed by the actions of those who were supposed to support you."

"Perhaps I should put a pebble in my shoe."

For a second Alexei thought she was serious. He shook his finger at her.

"There you go again," he said.

The ride to the Kremlin took about thirty minutes on a good day. Today, Moscow traffic was terrible. Even Vysotsky's escort had trouble getting through the mess. They arrived only minutes before the meeting was due to begin. Two uniformed guards stood outside the open doors of Orlov's office. Alexei saw that Volkov had arrived before him. He sat in a gilded chair in front of Orlov's desk. A second chair was empty.

"Wait out here," Vysotsky said to Valentina.

The guards closed the tall doors to the office behind him.

Orlov looked at his watch. "You are exactly on time, General. Please sit."

Alexei took a seat. His chair had a high, curved back and a red plush seat.

"General Volkov has been telling me an interesting story," Orlov said. "He says Major Antipov killed Major Rostov. That her actions led to the failure of the mission."

"He is lying, Mister President. He wishes to cover up the results of his orders. Major Rostov is the one responsible for the destruction of the archive. She tried to kill Major Antipov and was going to kill the Americans."

"He is the one who is lying," Volkov said. "Antipov took every opportunity to prevent Major Rostov from succeeding. She was protecting the American spy, her sister."

Orlov held up his hand. "Stop. I will not sit here and listen to this bickering. One of you is lying. I am going to find out who it is. General Vysotsky."

"Yes, Mister President."

"I saw Major Antipov outside. Bring her in."

Volkov said, "She doesn't belong here."

"Be quiet, General."

Alexei went to the doors and pushed one open. "Major Antipov. Come."

Valentina rose and limped into Orlov's office. She came to attention in front of his desk and saluted.

"At ease, Major. You are wounded?"

"Yes, Mister President. It's nothing."

"Sit."

"Sir."

Valentina sat down.

"Tell me what happened in Egypt."

"Yes, sir. Where would you like me to begin?"

"I have read the reports of General Volkov and General Vysotsky. Begin on the night you entered the pyramid. What were your instructions?"

"I was instructed to observe the actions of the American spies and to avoid intervention unless absolutely necessary."

"Your instructions were only to observe and gather information?"

"Yes, sir. If possible, I was to locate the records of the Atlantis civilization. The Americans had more information than we did. It made sense to follow them. Major Rostov and I observed them enter the pyramid in the afternoon during the regular tourist hours. That evening they returned. The guide they had employed earlier opened the gate to the entrance and let them in."

"What time was that?"

"About ten that night. The complex was deserted. Major Rostov and I followed them into the pyramid. The Americans had discovered and opened a hidden entrance to a system of tunnels. The tunnels led to a large chamber filled with the records we were seeking."

"Then what happened?"

"We disarmed them. Rostov told them to stand against a wall. I asked her what she intended to do. She was going to kill them. I asked her how she was going to explain the bodies. That is when she shot me."

"You are lying!" Volkov said.

Orlov looked at him. His voice was hard and cold as the frozen steppes of Siberia. "Be quiet. I will not ask you again."

He turned back to Valentina. "Continue, Major."

"It gets confusing after that. I was on the floor. Rostov started shooting at the Americans. One of her bullets struck the chemical lighting in the room. That's what started the fire. Rostov shot at them and they fired back. She was hit. As she went down her gun set off a trap that fell and killed her."

"General Volkov says Major Rostov told him you were obstructing her investigation. That you were doing it because your sister was part of the American team and that you were in contact with her."

"If she said that, she lied."

"You are a disgrace to your uniform," Volkov said. "You are a traitor. I will see you broken for what you just said."

Valentina flushed. "You don't scare me, General. You are a pedophile and a liar. I know about the little girls you take out to your dacha. Although I suspect President Orlov is unaware of your sexual preferences."

Alexei was surprised. He knew Volkov's dirty secret but he hadn't thought that Valentina did. He'd held back from using it against his rival except as a last resort. Now it was unnecessary. If Orlov believed her, Valentina had just sealed Volkov's fate. Whatever else he was, Orlov was a man who did not tolerate sexual deviancy.

"General Vysotsky. Is this true?"

"I hesitated to bring this to you without firm proof, Mister President. Yes, I believe it is true."

"General Volkov? Do you deny the accusation?"

"Of course I deny it. It's another one of her lies."

Orlov had been watching Volkov as he responded. Now he touched a button on his desk. The doors swung open. The two guards entered the room.

"Arrest General Volkov. Take him to Lefortovo. Put him in isolation."

Volkov's voice rose, a note of desperation creeping in. "Mister President, she is lying."

"Is she?" Orlov gestured to the guards. "Take him away."

They dragged Volkov out of the room, protesting. The doors closed behind them.

"I am sorry you had to go through this unpleasant experience, Valentina. May I call you Valentina?"

"Of course, Mister President." She smiled at him. "It's an honor."

"Your wound is healing?"

"Yes, sir."

"Others besides yourself observed Major Rostov's hostility toward you. I have a report from the captain of the *Tolstoy*. He has no love for the Americans but lays the blame for the damages to his ship primarily on Rostov."

"She provoked them by sabotaging their undersea vehicle."

"So he says. You have been very brave, my dear."

"I was only doing my duty."

Valentina cast her eyes down as she spoke. If Vysotsky hadn't known better, he would have thought her humility was real.

CHAPTER 55

In Virginia, Elizabeth eyed Nick and the others. The long flight from Egypt had left them looking like something Burps had dragged in from outside.

"You're certain nothing is left?"

"Not a chance," Nick said. "I've never seen anything burn as fast or as hot as that. Karimi said the heat brought down the roof. Everything is buried under tons of stone."

"Do we have any other leads we can follow? Selena?"

"There's nothing, Elizabeth. There might have been a clue in the undersea ruins but they're gone too. I had the stone in my hands but now it's gone. Whatever the secret was, it's lost."

"The French succeeded in translating the writing on the museum tablet. They're calling it a hoax."

"That doesn't surprise me," Selena said. "Anytime something new shows up challenging accepted dogma, people attack it. The French and everyone else will always resist any idea of an earlier civilization."

"General Karimi knows what happened," Nick said.

Elizabeth said, "He blamed the damage to the pyramid and the Sphinx on ISIS. The government is throwing money at him to protect what he calls 'Egypt's sacred history.' It's not to his advantage to say anything."

"No one would believe him anyway."

"There's been some interesting fallout in Russia," Elizabeth said. "Rostov's boss has been arrested. He's being accused of crimes against the state, whatever that means."

"It means Orlov blames him for what happened."

"That's my reading," Elizabeth said.

"Who's going to replace him?"

"No one knows. There are rumors Orlov may reconstitute the KGB and bring foreign and domestic security back under one roof. If he does, General Vysotsky could be the new director."

"Nothing ever changes, does it?" Lamont said.

"The Russians are consistent, if nothing else. In a way, it makes it easier to know what we're up against. Orlov is a throwback to the days of the Soviet Union. People don't want to admit it, but we're in a new Cold War."

"As long as it doesn't get hot," Ronnie said.

"It might get hot around here," Elizabeth said. "I've been subpoenaed."

"What? Why?" Nick asked.

"Congress is after DCI Hood. It's political. They're doing everything they can to discredit President Rice and his party before the election. Clarence is a sideshow that will play well in the media."

"Why you?"

"Because of this."

She passed over the picture from the tabloid.

"You can see what's happening. It's a perfect opportunity for the vultures in Congress who hate the idea that they can't control what we do. The president won't tell them what they want to know about our operations. They want to take down two birds with one stone, if you'll pardon the cliché. This picture is an excuse to start the hue and cry."

"Those assholes on the hill don't understand that we're fighting a war," Lamont said.

"They don't have to do the fighting," Ronnie said. "For them, it's a game they talk about in committees and watch on TV."

"This subpoena will cause problems," Elizabeth said. "I don't think any of you will get dragged in, but it's always possible. Meanwhile you deserve some time off. Enjoy it while you can. We're still in business and something's bound to come up."

"Are you and Hood seeing each other?" Selena asked.
Elizabeth blushed. Nick hadn't ever seen her do that before.

"He's only a friend," Elizabeth said.

CHAPTER 56

That night Nick and Selena lay in bed, resting after making love. It was a pleasant evening in Washington, the humidity low, the temperature hovering in the 70s. A breeze brought the smell of the Potomac through the open windows of the loft, cooling their overheated bodies. Somewhere on the river a boat horn sounded.

"I wish those ruins were still there to be explored," Selena said.

"At least we have pictures."

"It's not the same. Pictures will never be enough proof for people who don't want to believe Atlantis ever existed. All they have to do is claim they were faked."

"The French have that tablet. That should be enough to make people want to follow up."

"Everyone thinks that tablet is a hoax."

"How do they explain the fact that it weighs a lot less than it should?"

"They haven't, yet. I suppose they'll analyze it and come up with something. But with nothing to back it up it will end up being dismissed as an oddity. Like I said, a hoax."

"What about the Egyptians?" Nick asked. "There could be something left in that room. Fragments of the stone. Something that could be studied, analyzed."

"They'll never look for it," Selena said. "Even if there is something there, it's crushed under tons of rock. Besides, they don't want to find anything that threatens their interpretation of history. No one will ever be able to prove Atlantis was real."

"We know it was real. I guess that has to be enough. Why don't you blow up one of those pictures and frame it? Put it on the wall. Maybe that stone face. Or that picture you took in Paris of the tablet."

"Like another piece of art?"

"Why not?"

"One thing that bothers me is that no one is taking the language on that tablet seriously. It's a precursor of Linear A. It should be studied."

"Write a paper about it."

"It won't do any good. Once something is identified as a hoax, everything about it is dismissed."

"Even with your credentials?"

She was silent.

After a few minutes Nick said, "Are you still thinking about that tablet?"

"I was thinking about Valentina. I wonder how she's doing."

"Oh."

"What am I supposed to do about her?"

"There isn't anything to do. She's loyal to her country. She's a lot like you, really."

"You think so?"

"I do. You even look sort of the same. Something in the way you both move. The way you do the same things sometimes."

"Like what?"

"Haven't you seen her brush her hair away from her forehead? Just like you do."

"Now that you mention it. I wonder how she really feels about me?"

"She tried to get her gun to you. That tells you something."

"I wonder if I'll see her again."

"You keep crossing paths," Nick said.

"We can't seem to get the Russians out of our lives."

"We won't, as long as we're working for Harker."

"That's another thing. I've thought a lot about quitting. But I can't do it now, not when Elizabeth is under attack. It wouldn't be right. Besides, if I quit I'll never see Valentina again."

"We'll both know when it's time."

"Would you quit if I did?"

"I don't know."

"At least you're honest about it."

"I'd be lying if I said I never think about it."

"Every time we go out on a mission, I'm not sure we're coming back. I feel like we're tempting fate."

"Nobody lives forever," Nick said.

New Releases...

Be the first to know when I have a new book coming out by subscribing to my newsletter. No spam or busy emails, only a brief announcement now and then. Just click on the link below. You can unsubscribe at any time...

http://alexlukeman.com/contact.html#newsletter

The Project Series:

White Jade
The Lance
The Seventh Pillar
Black Harvest
The Tesla Secret
The Nostradamus File
The Ajax Protocol
The Eye of Shiva
Black Rose
The Solomon Scroll
The Russian Deception
The Atlantis Stone

Reviews by readers are welcome!
You can contact me at: **alex@alexlukeman.com**. I promise
to get back to you.
My website is: **www.alexlukeman.com**

NOTES

I always backup my stories with facts and elements of truth. When it comes to Atlantis and the history of Egypt there are many possible truths, speculations and theories to choose from.

For example, reliable scientific examination of the Sphinx reveals patterns of wear on the stone that could only have been caused by exposure to years of heavy rains. It has been many thousands of years since Egypt had that kind of rainfall. It would have ended long before the various dates given for construction of the Sphinx and the pyramids.

The Sphinx is supposed to have been constructed by Khufu at the same time as the great pyramid. The story of finding a commentary saying the Sphinx was buried in sand up to its head before the great pyramid was built comes from the nineteenth century. It has been dismissed as historical revisionism, but that may be part of a consistent pattern of denial by the Egyptian Ministry of antiquities when it comes to any challenge of the accepted timeline.

No one can really trust records left by the pharaohs. It was common practice to erase the achievements of their predecessors and take credit for themselves. Is it inconceivable that one of them claimed credit for the Sphinx even if he had nothing to do with its construction? In fact there are unresolved arguments about which Pharaoh may have been responsible.

There are many unexplained mysteries about the pyramids. The case can be made that they were never originally built as tombs. If the pyramids were not tombs, what were they for? If the dating of the Sphinx is called into question, so is the timeline for the pyramids. If they are much earlier than supposed, who built them?

How were the elaborate hieroglyphic decorations created inside the pyramids done without leaving smoke stains on the walls? What did the artists use for light? Some believe the pyramids generated energy and that this energy was used to power light for the painters.

There are indeed hidden chambers in and near the Sphinx. New sonar scan technology recently revealed a sealed entrance to a tunnel in the great pyramid. There are many known underground tunnels in the Giza complex. Most have been sealed since they were built and have not been opened. The ones that are open cannot be toured by the public.

An opening was discovered in the left hind quarter of the Sphinx years ago during an early restoration. It led to a tunnel ending in a wall. The tunnel was then blocked off with an iron gate. Photos still exist. The opening in the side of the Sphinx was sealed.

The Egyptian Ministry of Antiquities does not permit exploration of the hidden tunnels or chambers. All suggestions that the pyramids or the Sphinx are older than the third century BCE are brushed aside as absurd. No one wants to change the accepted historical timeline regardless of what scientific proof may be offered. Contrary evidence is routinely denied.

The information in this book about Plato is correct. The historian Crantor was an actual person who did write that he had seen pillars with the history of Atlantis written on them.

The story of Atlantis captures the imagination. There are serious researchers who believe Atlantis existed, although indisputable proof has not yet been found. It presents one of the great unknowns of Western civilization. Several locations for the vanished civilization have been suggested, among them the Azores.

The Azores were formed by volcanic action and the region is still seismically active, as is the Mediterranean. A Portuguese fisherman claimed to have discovered and scanned an undersea pyramid off the coast of Terciara. If there are any actual underwater ruins, they've been down there for a long, long time.

The weapons used in the story are real. The Russian APS rifle is a brilliant piece of weapons engineering. The H&K underwater pistol carried by Lamont is as described and must be sent back to the factory for reloading. Shooting something underwater is a major challenge.

As for moving tons of stone through the air with a simple push, modern science is now beginning to touch the possibility of creating devices capable of defeating gravity.

Thanks for reading *The Atlantis Stone*.

ACKNOWLEDGMENTS

My wife, Gayle, as always. I'd have a hard time doing this without her support.

Special thanks to Gloria Lakritz, Paul Madsen, Tina Malone and Eric Vollbreght.

Thanks to Neil Jackson for his excellent cover.

Wikipedia Commons for the public domain image of the interior of the pyramid.

Finally, thanks to you, the reader. You are why I write...

ABOUT THE AUTHOR

Alex Lukeman writes action/adventure thrillers featuring a covert intelligence unit called the PROJECT. Alex is a former Marine and psychotherapist and uses his experience of the military and human nature to inform his work. He likes riding old, fast motorcycles and playing guitar, usually not at the same time. You can email him at alex@alexlukeman.com. He loves hearing from readers and promises he will get back to you.

http://www.alexlukeman.com